TUTANKHAMUN:
HE IS BORN
(Book 1)

To David and
Partner - Enjoy
Aisha.

A.D.P. SORISI

ISBN-13: 978-1544797946

British Library Cataloguing in Publication Data.
A CIP catalogue record for this book is available from the
British Library.

DEDICATION

For my great nephews
James Willcox, Taha Eid,
Nouredine Haji & Joshua Tiwari-Hope

And great nieces
Mariam Eid & Jessica Weston

THE RISING STARS OF THE FUTURE

ACKNOWLEDGMENTS

Many thanks to:

Front cover: Ronnie Rayner Larter

Suzan Collins for her support and direction

Tutankhamun Trilogy

Historical Characters

The following characters in this work are real people who lived in Ancient Egyptian times and held the positions ascribed to them in this work.

Pharaoh Akhenaten – fathered Tutankhamun

Nefertiti – wife of Pharaoh Akhenaten with whom he fathered six daughters

Lady Kiya – mother of Tutankhamun and Second Wife of the Pharaoh

Maya – wet-nurse to Prince Tut, elevated by Pharaoh Tut to Treasurer and Overseer of the Palace of Eernity (Royal Cemeteries)

Pharaoh Amenhotep III – known as the Great Memnon; father of Akhenaten and grandfather to Tut

The Lady Tiya – wife of Amenhotep III, mother of Akhenaten and grandmother to Tut
Nakhtmia (Nakht) – Tut's friend and mentor (gifts were found in Tut's tomb inscribed with Nakht's name)

Ankhen – youngest daughter of Akhenaten and Nefertiti, Tut's half-sister and later his Queen

Ay – Vizier (Prime minister) to Akhenaten and later also to Pharaoh Tut

Horemheb – Commander-in-Chief of Egypt; son-in-law to Ay and brother-in-law to Nefertiti

All other characters are from the author's imagination although such positions must have existed.

Egyptian Middle Kingdom Calendar

AKET: First Season. The period when the Nile floods; caused by heavy rain and melting snow in the Ethiopian Mountains.

The months consist of 30 days each and a week consists of 10 days. The working week is 9 days with the 10th day off for visiting family.

Month

1 of Aket	Tekh
2	Menhet
3	Hwt-hwr
4	Ka-hr-ka

PERET: Second Season. The period when the Nile flood water retreats leaving a rich and fertile layer of black silt. Ideal for planting.

5 First of Peret	Sf-bdt
6 Second of Peret	Rekh wer
7 Third of Peret	Rekh neds
8 Fourth of Peret	Renwet

SHEMU: Third season, 'low water'. The period of harvest when Nile lilies are plentiful. Thought to be the period within which Pharaoh Tutankhamun died.

9 First of Shemu	Hnsw
10 Second of Shemu	Hnt-htj
11 Third of Shemu	Ipt-hmt
12 Fourth of Shemu	Wep-renpet

Five days, dedicated to the gods, were added to make the year 365 days.

Chapter 1

It was Menhet, the second month of Aket, the season of inundation when the life giving waters of the Nile flood the flat desert land, enriching it, ensuring good growing condition for another year.

"*Arghhhhhhhh!*" A heart-rending scream emanated from the arbour situated at the northern end of the Second Wife's royal garden, surrounded by trees and scented flowering bushes.

Inside the structure of lightweight poles and greenery the air was thick with pain and the smell of blood. In the centre of this childbed retreat was the Lady Kiya, the King's favourite wife, squatting over two large bricks with a gap between. Her hands were upon her knees. Two older women squatted either side of her, supporting her elbow and forearm.

In front of her, also squatting, was the midwife. Perspiration rolled down Lady Kiya's face and naked body. She had been in labour since sunset. She had had a compress round the lower half of her swollen belly with the usual layer of straw and reeds beneath it to free the child from the womb. The midwife had applied a douche of warm oil and the Lady Kiya had inhaled the cool northerly breeze which, being the breath of Amun, should have eased the pain but did not. Then her weary mind remembered the god of the land was no longer Amun but Aten. From the faint light filtering through the white linen awning she sensed morning was near. All her thoughts were for the wellbeing of the child.

"Just one more push" she heard the midwife repeat for the hundredth time. When will it end? she thought as another spasm of pain rocked through her tired frame.

"It's coming," hissed the midwife. She could see the head. She had her orders. If it was a boy it had to come out with the feeding cord round its neck. If a girl it could live. The midwife felt a pang of fear as, with a final agonising scream, the baby slid into her hands.

Time seemed to stand still. How could she kill this beautiful, perfectly formed infant? But it was his life or hers. She dare not go against her instructions. Just as she was about to wrap the cord around the child's neck her assistant, to the right of the now unconscious mother, whispered harshly, "the King's physician."

The midwife grabbed a clean piece of linen and started wiping the newborn.

A tall, well-built man, dressed in a long robe with a clean shaven head and permanent frown on an otherwise pleasing countenance, looked at the child, barely bigger than the midwife's hands. The midwife deftly cut the cord and the baby let out a lusty cry as it drew its first breath.

The man smiled. "The King will be pleased. A son at last."

He beckoned to the wet-nurse to take the child. "Take good care of him."

Having noted the mother's body and heavy loss of blood, he shook his head. "The King will be unhappy at the loss of his favourite wife. Do what you can and keep me informed of her condition."

With that he left the arbour taking care not to get blood on the edge of his white robe.

The prone body of the Lady Kiya was washed and dressed in a fresh gown before being placed on the bed situated in the middle of the arbour. The sun was up and a cool breeze was blowing through. No one of any importance noticed the lack of a placenta in the birthing debris.

The King, having been given the news, rushed to Lady Kiya's side. He smoothed her damp hair and kissed her pale cheeks, feeling her shallow breath on his face. He thanked her for his long awaited son and mentioned all the honours he would shower on her, jewels, her own palace, gold, silver, anything her heart desired. Then he left her to sleep.

The midwife reported the birth personally to Queen Nefertiti, stressing the condition of the Lady Kiya. The look on the Queen's face confirmed what the midwife feared – she would need to keep out of the Queen's sight for her own safety.

The Lady Kiya never regained consciousness. By the following morning her spirit had slipped quietly out of her decaying-placenta-poisoned body but it refused to move away from her child. She had personally chosen the wet nurse, Maya. Maya was a good and loyal servant to her and whom she was sure would love the child as her own. The wet nurse had had a stillborn child a short time ago, so her milk was plentiful and her heart was seeking a child to nurture.

When news of Lady Kiya's death reached her, the Queen took some solace from the death of her rival. In the past year or so the Queen had felt she was losing the affection of her beloved husband Akhenaten. She had borne him six daughters while all her prayers for a son had gone unheeded.

She was resourceful enough, she decided, to ensure the boy did not survive infancy. She slaked her anger by giving the order for the permanent removal of the midwife.

Chapter 2

"Father, you are the King's Vizier, the most powerful man in Egypt after Pharaoh and currently next in line to the throne, so what are we going to do about the Boy? He is already two weeks old."

"Calm yourself daughter, remember your husband, the Pharaoh, fathered that child."

"I have my doubts about that. How could he father a son with her but not with me?" said Queen Nefertiti bitterly.

"Nef, you know full well it would be almost impossible for another man to have had carnal knowledge of the Lady Kiya. Do not let jealousy cloud your judgment."

"But Father, you and my sister's husband Horemheb, Commander in Chief, deserve to be Pharaoh after my Akhenaten, not that spewing infant! The two of you have successfully been sharing power with my beloved; caring and nurturing the country for many years."

"Nef, it is the gods, not us, who decide our fate."

"Are we to do nothing about the child?"

"You know as well as I that infant diseases, even in a palace, may well take care of the problem. Let us wait. If he gets to the age of six when his kingship training begins in earnest, we shall speak again on the matter. Until then put it out of your mind."

"Easier said than done Father. You know I respect your counsel but cannot agree with you on this occasion. Inaction is not an option for me."

"Nef, you have always been headstrong. I indulged it because I believed it was a good trait for a future queen to possess but you must, at this age, have regard to the greater good – not least the needs of your husband to provide a male heir to carry on his dynasty."

"Father, I know my husband and understand him better than even he believes. My actions will be for the good of the Dynasty."

The Vizier shook his head sadly and decided to say no more on the matter.

As Nefertiti made her way back to her quarters she pondered what she could do to give nature a helping hand.

If that feeble minded midwife had carried out my instructions this would not now be a problem. It is small comfort knowing she is in an unmarked grave, thought the Queen. She resolved to put the thought of what to do about the child away until opportunity to take action presented itself.

Although Pharaoh Akhenaten, also known by his throne name Amenhotep IV, dearly loved and respected his Queen, he had his own means of knowing what was going on in her quarters. The servant girl Kara now reported to him that the Queen had been in conference with her father Ay, the Vizier, this very day.

The body of Lady Kiya was with the embalmers and Akhenaten had hoped to think about the safety of the child once the mother had been buried but he decided to take action in that regard now. He sent a trusted messenger to his parents in Thebes asking that an apartment be made ready for their grandson, Tutanaten, as well as his wet nurse and servants.

The King suspected his revered father, Amenhotep III, regretted giving up the throne, since Akhenaten's first act was to change the country's age old religion. However, the King knew having a baby in her home again, after so many years, would bring joy to his mother's life and, he hoped, a new interest to brighten his father's old age.

Nefertiti never allowed his mother, the Lady Tiya, to spend time with her granddaughters because, she claimed, of the rift between father and son but the King was certain the child would grow up safe, loved and well-nourished in his parents' home. He acted immediately and word was sent to Maya, Tut's wet nurse, to make ready for the move.

Before Akhenaten, taken up with affairs of State, could tell the Queen of his decision, she learned of it from her head housekeeper, Polydama, who was cousin to the palace head housekeeper.

That evening as they lay together in each other's arms, Nefertiti raised her long graceful neck and petite head which had been resting on her husband's clean shaven chest, and looked at his face. His eyes were closed but she knew he was not asleep.

"Why are you sending the child away?" she asked.

The King took a deep breath, opened his eyes and returned her gaze. Diplomacy of the highest order was needed.

"Nef, I know your heart suffered when I paid attention to the Lady Kiya. You surely understand it was nothing to do with love but duty. I needed a son to carry on our dynasty. My heart belongs to you and our daughters. A man has to make the woman he hopes to bear him a child feel special, happy and content so that she bears him a healthy, happy child. That has always been my philosophy. You know it to be true. I have done no less for you."

"That is what hurts. You have ever only treated me that way" replied Nefertiti.

"I am sending the child away because I want your mind to be at peace. The child's only importance is as Prince Regent and not because Lady Kiya, now departed from this life, was his mother."

Nefertiti, tears in her eyes, laid her head again on her beloved husband's chest. She could find no fault with the words he had spoken, only comfort. Yet she felt the need to know how the child would fare. She decided to have one of her servants go with the Prince's retinue to keep her, the Queen, informed. With this thought she fell into a dreamless sleep.

As Nefertiti's eyelids fluttered open the next morning she noted her husband had already left for his rooms. She stretched her slender limbs lazily as she thought about the matters to be dealt with that day.

Having heard her mistress stir, her hand maiden entered the partially opened door to the bedchamber with fresh towels and a jug of warm water and another of cold water. The Queen sat up and looked around her chamber with satisfaction. She loved her palace in the new capital they had moved to from Memphis. She had designed her own and her daughters quarters to ensure sufficient storage finery and clothing, hats and shoes as well as towels and bedding.

The fine, white, linen curtains wafted gently. She walked to her veranda stretching and taking in a lungful of air coming off the mountains. Looking at the Nile gently flowing by, its flood waters rising every day, she noted it was already busy with boatmen plying their trade. The white sails, moving in the morning breeze, looked like giant herons paying homage to her. On the far bank, lined with date palm trees, branches waving gently, she could see the semi naked *fellahin* women and slaves in bright headdresses fetching water.

Turning back into her room she beckoned her handmaiden with a slight incline of her head.

After her ablutions her body was massaged with sandalwood oil before she was assisted into her close fitting gown of gold. Nefertiti sat before a large gold edged mirror with herons in flight etched in the far left hand corner, applied kohl to her eyes, henna to her lips and coiffed her hair in its usual style. She silently thanked her mother for ensuring she was schooled in the art of making the best of her looks. She was trained by the beautician in her father's household. Her mother taught her to rely on herself in all matters concerning care of her body and looks. Her hand maiden freshened up the henna on the Queen's finger and toe nails and assisted with her footwear.

The Queen then turned to the ornate small table

on which her breakfast had been set. On the matter of food the Queen was a creature of habit, habits which only varied slightly when she was with child. Breakfast consisted of exactly two sycamore figs, two dates and six large grapes together with a thick slice of bread spread thinly with honey and cheese. All this was followed by a glass of pomegranate juice.

Her trusted head housekeeper, Polydama, whom the Queen referred to as Poly for convenience, was in the anteroom awaiting the Queen's pleasure. The handmaiden ushered Poly in when the Queen had finished her breakfast.

"Ah, Poly, I seek your assistance. Which of my hand maidens do you consider can be trusted to take on a delicate assignment?"

Poly frowned, thinking. "Perhaps if Your Majesty could give me some idea of the nature of the assignment…?"

"I need someone to join the baby prince's household so as to keep me informed of his health and progress."

After a moment's thought Poly replied, "I would suggest Swnwt. She has been in your service since the age of seven and is now fifteen. She is a quick learner and I have noticed she does not join in when the other servants are gossiping. Her mother lives in the palace with rooms in the retired servant's quarters, something which could prove useful to Your Majesty should Swnwt need persuading to do your bidding."

"Then arrange it, Poly. I require monthly reports unless the child falls ill then I want to know immediately. We will deal with housekeeping matters on your return."

Poly bowed slightly and left.

Having dealt satisfactorily with that item, the Queen retired to her writing room to sort State correspondence assigned to her by her beloved husband.

Poly, having taken leave of her mistress, went in search of Swnwt to instruct her on her new duties. Swnwt was currently on loan to the palace head housekeeper, Poly's cousin, who needed someone discreet to help look after the mistress of a visiting dignitary. Word was sent to Swnwt and before long she knocked on Poly's office door.

"You wanted to see me?" said Swnwt. "Is something wrong?"

"No. I wanted to inform you of an elevation in your status. Sit down."

Swnwt, alarmed and apprehensive, sat on the edge of her chair. She had never heard of handmaidens being 'elevated' before - whatever that meant.

"I take it you are aware the Pharaoh's young wife gave birth to a son?"

"Yes. I heard she died in childbirth."

"That is so. The child is alive and being cared for by his wet nurse Maya. The King is sending the baby Prince and his household to his parents in Thebes. The Queen instructs that you accompany the Prince as a handmaiden to the wet-nurse."

"I had no idea the Queen knew of my existence. Why me?"

"I recommended you for the position."

"Why would you do that?"

"I have noticed you are a hard worker and you do not gossip with the other maids."

"What would the Queen want of me?"

"She requires you to provide full monthly reports on how the child fares. If he is ill she wants to know as soon as possible."

"How am I to inform her if I am in Thebes?"

"You will be given homing birds trained to return to the Queen's balcony. They can be housed with the other birds at the Small Palace, used for a similar purpose - to get messages to the King here at the palace. You have an elderly mother living in the retired servant's quarters, I believe."

Swnwt shook her head in the affirmative.

"You will be allowed to visit her one day in every thirty. If you need to send an urgent message - concerning the child's health - you can say it is for your mother. Messages will always be brought to me. When you come to visit make sure you report to me first."

Swnwt sat wringing her hands, her young face, hinting at the beauty yet to blossom, a picture of fear.

"What is the matter?" asked Poly.

"Suppose I do not wish such a post? I have not the cunning for it."

"No one says no to the Queen! Have you no love for your mother? Would you have her turned out of the palace along with you?"

"No." With tears of frustration and worry Swnwt confirmed she would do as the Queen commands.

"Good. I will see to the arrangements and let you know the time for moving. Go tell your mother of your good fortune."

Chapter 3

Maya, a comely woman in her early twenties, still carrying baby fat from her recent pregnancy, felt the responsibility for the future Pharaoh very keenly. There was a point during the birthing, just before the physician arrived, when she feared for the baby's life. The mid-wife had had such a strange look on her face as she stared at the newborn. Maya shook her head as though to clear her thoughts and started to pack.

They were moving in three days' time to Thebes, to the home of Amenhotep III and his wife the Lady Tiya. Maya hoped they were kind people. She made a mental note to arrange for one of the palace scribes to label the boxes.

The following day the palace head housekeeper visited Maya.

"I am here to explain the move to Thebes," she said. The woman was built like a man, tall and solid, with broad shoulders and strong arms. Yet her manner was maternal.

"Your task in the Prince's household at Thebes will be as it has been here - to feed, care for and keep the young Prince safe. There will be servants to do everything else. You will have a room adjoining the child's nursery, and there will be rooms in the same wing for two hand- maidens to assist you with the care of the child. House servants will be responsible for cooking, washing and cleaning for the Prince's household.

"The head housekeeper of the household you are joining will see to quarters for them and will be responsible for such staff. In addition to your existing handmaiden Zelda another, named Swnwt, will be joining the Prince's household."

"Can you tell me something about Swnwt? I have not come across her in the palace."

"She is a sturdy, pleasant, hard working girl of fifteen who can be trusted. That is all you need to know," was the reply.

The head housekeeper's voice had taken on a steely edge that had not been there before. Maya decided to keep an eye on Swnwt. She asked the housekeeper to arrange for a scribe to label the boxes.

Late on the last night in the palace at the new Capital, Akhenhaten, the King, came to see his son.

He had promised Nefertiti that he would visit the child only once a year, on the date of his birth, until the Prince reached the age of six, when he would return to the palace for kingship training.

Maya, on seeing the King, stepped in the shadows.

The King bent down and kissed the sleeping child

on the forehead, sighed deeply and left.

The Lady Kiya had forewarned Maya of danger from the Queen if she provided the King with an heir but Maya could sense that was not the only source of danger.

Ay, the King's Vizier, and Horemheb, the King's Commander-in-Chief both came to visit the child before his departure to Thebes, commenting on how happy and well-nourished he looked. Maya remained in the shadow.

Horemheb looked at Ay.

"What are you thinking?" asked Ay, suspicion in his voice.

"It would be so easy to end this now. All I have to do is put my hand over the child's nose and mouth. It would not take long to put out that little life."

Before Ay could respond Horemheb moved forward and was about to place his large, rough-looking hand over the sleeping baby's nose and mouth. Then, as though bitten, Horemheb jumped back, a look akin to fear in his eyes.

Ay's anger at Horemheb's action was palpable but he was taken aback by that fleeting look of fear. Horemheb, nursing his right arm whispered, "There is strong magic at work protecting this child," as he backed away from the crib.

"What do you mean by going against my instructions?" hissed Ay once they were in the corridor. "Do you wish to see both of us beheaded? What do you mean by 'strong magic'? What did you see?"

"It is not what I saw. It is what I felt, as though some demon had hold of my arm. The touch was cold yet burned like fire."

"Did you not realise that the wet-nurse was nearby? Were you planning to despatch her also? Such recklessness does not sit well with your position. Heed my words and leave the matter to the gods."

Horemheb did not agree with the Vizier's strategy of doing nothing. Yet he could not afford to openly defy Ay. He therefore apologised for his momentary lapse whilst still intending to continue his efforts to end the child's life.

Maya had frozen on the spot at Horemheb's forward movement towards the crib. She had sensed a shadow bear down on Horemheb's outstretched arm before it could reach the sleeping babe. She saw him jump back in surprise and fear. Maya had the distinct impression Lady Kiya was in the room.

How can that be? she wondered. Movement returned to her limbs when she realised the men had left. She crept to the crib and examined the boy. No mark on him. She gave a silent prayer of thanks.

She felt ashamed at not having responded to the threat to Tut and resolved to ensure they were well guarded on the journey to Thebes.

Maya woke her maid Zelda and instructed her to stay with the sleeping child until she, Maya, returned. Maya made her way to the quarters of the Captain of the King's Elite Guards. The palace hallways were dimly lit as she hurried on her errand, her heart pounding at the thought of how easy it would be for someone to despatch her with one stroke of a dagger. Such a thought had never occurred to her before. She made a desperate effort to control her growing fear and almost ran to the guards' room.

She explained to the sentry on guard duty who she was and was taken to the Captain. As though to make up for her earlier loss of will- power Maya felt a surge of confidence and, facing the Captain, she boldly explained, "I am concerned to know the steps being taken to protect the Prince on the journey to Thebes on the morrow."

The Captain, a battle-scarred, seasoned fighter in his thirties, looked at the young woman before him who was trying hard to project a brave, confident front. He realised her job was a dangerous one. She could, he reasoned, lose her own life. Yet he sensed she was only concerned with the welfare of her royal charge.

"My apologies, Lady," he said. "I should have acquainted you with the military plans for the journey. Please, sit. I will explain."

Maya, relaxing her rigid posture slightly, sat on the stool offered. The Captain pulled a map from the side of his desk, opened it and showed Maya the planned route.

He explained the number of guards assigned the task of protecting the Prince on the journey. "There will also be trainee soldiers around the Prince's carriage the whole time in case of attack from within the group, with fighting men on the perimeter in case of attack from without."

"From within the group?" muttered Maya.

"We must overlook nothing," said the Captain.

"Thank you. Will you be accompanying us?"

"No. My second-in-command, an able soldier, will be in charge of the detail. My place is here, protecting the Pharaoh." The Captain called one of his guards. "Escort this lady back to the royal nursery."

Maya thought about protesting, but instead thanked the Captain.

Meanwhile, in another part of the palace, Queen

Nefertiti was, through her trusted servant Poly, giving orders for the despatch of the young Prince to the netherworld. The opportunity to attack while the party travelled to Thebes was too good to be missed. Earlier that evening on being questioned by Poly, Swnwt confirmed she was travelling in the coach behind the Prince's having been told that Maya and Zelda would be looking after the babe on the journey.

The Vice-Captain introduced himself to Maya when he came to escort them to their conveyance, handing her a 'gift' from the Captain. Maya looked at the 'gift' and then at the Vice-Captain questioningly.

"The Captain thought it may be needed for your protection. Open it."

Maya unwrapped the linen around the object and gave a sharp intake of breath as she stared at the small, plain dagger resting in her hand. She looked at the soldier in front of her. "I would never be able to use this! I have never so much as said a harsh word to anyone in my life. How can the Captain expect me to use this to defend myself?"

"He thought it a prudent gift since we have not been given the number of trainees requested."

"How many have we been given?" asked Maya.

"One," replied the Vice-Captain, trying to sound

positive.

Maya shook her head in disbelief but secreted the weapon, wrapped in linen, in her cloak pocket.

The travellers set off at dawn. The two coaches were followed by servants on foot and many carts carrying luggage, water, cooking utensils and food as well as feed for the horses and donkeys.

As the coaches rattled away from the city Maya noted shabby dwellings clustered together wherever there was a source of water. Chickens, goats and small donkeys wandered around the dwellings while naked children ran about playing. The older inhabitants, mainly women were tending small vegetable patches near the waterside. The very old, of which she only noted one or two, sat in the shade keeping an eye on the playing children. Maya called to the soldier riding nearby.

"Who are these people?"

"They are the *fellahin*, peasants. They live off the land, moving from time to time following the water," he replied.

As the sun rose higher in the clear blue sky, the heat seared the ground. Baby Tut became fractious. Maya disrobed him, patting his body with a damp cloth to cool him down. Zelda sat opposite, fanning the child.

As they were thus engaged a raggedly-dressed *fellahin* jumped unto the slow-moving coach, pulling open the door. Maya looked up to see the glint of a dagger in the sunlight. She twisted round, plunging her own dagger into the heart of the attacker before he could bring down his raised arm. He fell back with a look of surprise and disbelief on his face.

When the coach came to a stop she noticed a young man of about fifteen years old with broad shoulders and a colourful feather at the back of his head, jump off his horse and inspect the body of the attacker. The Vice-Captain and other guards were now also surrounding the coach. The young man with the feather in his hair looked up at the trembling Maya, her blood stained hand and drawn face, with respect.

"Your first kill?"

She shook her head, unable to speak.

"It was fortunate the Captain thought to make you a present of that dagger," said the Vice-Captain.

"I never thought I would be able to take the life of another human being," replied Maya in a trembling voice.

Zelda was sitting wide-eyed and clearly traumatised by the occurrence. Baby Tut was waving his naked arms and legs, gurgling happily.

"The attacker is dead. He has nothing on his person to identify who he is. I will enquire of the servants." This was said to the Vice-Captain. Turning to Maya he said, "I am Nakhtmia, trainee soldier."

"Are you the one attached to the Prince's coach?"

"Yes," replied Nakhtmia.

"How is it you did not see the attacker?" she asked angrily.

"I was a little way back and was galloping to your coach when I saw the man fall," replied Nakht.

"I will stay with the Prince's coach" said the Vice-Captain in an effort to calm the situation.

Maya then noticed Swnwt who had, when her conveyance stopped, rushed towards Maya, side stepping the still-bleeding corpse.

"What can I do to help?" asked Swnwt anxiously.

"Take Zelda. Get her a drink and keep an eye on her. She witnessed her whole family murdered before being brought to Egypt. This will take time for her to overcome. I will need your help when we get to Thebes. That is all for now."

The Small Palace on the edge of Thebes was ablaze with light as the Prince's household trundled into the front court yard. At the entrance to the building stood an elegantly-clad older woman.

Maya guessed the matronly figure standing beside her was her head housekeeper since she was giving instructions to the household staff who seemed to appear from nowhere.

The Captain of the Household Guards came forward and spoke to the King's Vice-Captain. He then returned to the Lady of the House and conversed with her before accompanying her to the carriage in which her royal grandson was being swaddled against the cool of the evening. The Captain opened the carriage door and assisted Maya down before picking up the baby and showing him to the Lady Tiya.

"May I present Prince Tutanaten and his wet-nurse," he said, looking towards Maya.

"I am Maya."

The older woman with a beautiful face smiled at Maya. "I am the Lady Tiya, mother of Pharaoh Akhenaten. I am so happy to welcome you to my home. I understand your coach was attacked. You must be exhausted. Come with me. My housekeeper will see to everything."

"I have two handmaidens to assist with the care of the Prince. One is particularly affected by the attack. May I ask that she be taken to our rooms and be given something warm to drink. Swnwt, the other handmaiden, will assist in getting our belongings in while I see to the Prince."

The Lady Tiya gave instructions to her housekeeper then took Maya by the elbow and guided her into the palace to a comfortable room where a light supper was set out.

Maya felt grateful that baby Tut was suckling well and her milk was satisfying him. The King's physician had given the chief cook orders that Maya was to have the best foods to eat to ensure a plentiful supply of rich milk for the Prince. From the spread before her, the Lady Tiya was of the same mind.

The Lady Tiya sat quietly opposite Maya as she fed and then laid the baby beside her. Tiya rang a small bell standing on the nearby table and two maids entered, one carrying a bowl and the other a pitcher of water and a towel.

Maya washed her hands and face and smoothed her wet hands over her sleek, straight black hair.

"I am delighted to welcome you and the young Prince's household. Thank you for saving my grandson from an assassin's knife. You acted promptly and with great courage, I understand."

Maya looked at the Lady Tiya in surprise. "I am not courageous. I did not think. I just knew I had to save Tut. I drew the dagger without realising what I was doing and before I could blink the attacker lay dead. I never dreamt I could kill anyone. Yet for this child beside me I realised, in that moment, I would move mountains if called upon to do so for his safety."

"Come, let us have our first meal together. My husband is in his quarters. He will see his grandson by and by. We need to get you weary travellers abed."

"What of the soldiers that accompanied us?" asked Maya.

"They are being seen to. They will rest here tonight and make the journey back in the morning. A message has been sent to my son confirming your safe arrival. Let me show you your quarters. We can discuss housekeeping matters another time."

On his return to the palace at Akhenhaten the Captain informed his Pharaoh of the attempt on the Prince's life and the wet-nurse's prompt action in despatching the assassin.

"Your Vice-Captain informs me no-one in the detail knows the attacker. He was dressed in rags, with no distinguishing marks. So far it is proving impossible to trace his family or acquaintances. The Vice-Captain informed the old King's Captain who confirm steps will be taken to tighten security around the Small Palace."

"So we have no idea who instructed him?" mused the King.

"It was impossible to keep the move a secret," responded the Captain. "He could have been enlisted by any number of factions."

"Ensure there is sufficient support provided to my father's Household Guards to protect my son. Speak with our Treasurer and your counterpart of Father's Household Guards."

"It shall be as you command." Bowing the Captain left the King.

That evening as the King lay beside his Queen she looked at him enquiringly. "Something is worrying you more than usual. What is it?" she asked.

He looked down at her upturned face and smiled. "You are always able to read me."

"I have been married to you since I was a girl of fifteen. You are my world," she replied. "What is troubling you?"

"There was an attack on the Prince's life yesterday." He felt his wife's body stiffen.

"What occurred?"

"A man dressed as a *fellahin* attempted to kill the child but his wet-nurse was armed and managed to stab the attacker in the heart. She clearly has a mother's instinct towards the Prince."

"Do you have any idea who the attacker was?"

"No. Nor on whose order he was acting."

The Queen's body relaxed and she laid her head on her husband's chest.

"Let me help you forget your cares for a while," she whispered.

Chapter 4

The Small Palace at Thebes was much smaller than that at Akhenhaten. Whilst well-furnished, there was no display of opulence such as existed at the royal palace.

The outer walls that surrounded the palace were high, thick and well-built. The large wooden gates allowing access were solid and covered in intricate carvings warding off evil. The outer courtyard had a water fountain and date palm trees provided shade for the guards, whose numbers had increased with the arrival of the young Prince.

The palace itself was built around an inner courtyard where exotic, scented flowers grew tended by many gardeners, under the watchful eye of a tall, broad shouldered man with a weather beaten, handsome face.

In the centre of this inner space stood a large, beautiful fountain. In the pond surrounding the fountain were well tended, colourful water lilies with fishes lurking under the shade the lily pads afforded. To the back of the palace was a large open green area. An avenue of flowering trees were to the left of the open space, with ornate seating provided at intervals. To the rear of the avenue was a small orchard of fruit trees and to the right was the vegetable garden which provided most of the fresh produce needed by the household. Irrigation ditches, fed by a large container at the rear, criss-crossed the rear gardens. The container was filled morning and evening by the servants fetching water from the Nile, reached through a stout wooden door in the rear wall of the palace.

In the evening when the gardeners watered the avenue of trees and the green area, the air was filled with the scent of grass mixed with the perfume the flowers, giving off an exotic aroma such as Maya had not experienced since leaving King Tushratta's palace. It stirred vague memories of walking with Princess Kiya in King Tushratta's Mediterranean gardens.

As the weeks passed Tiya grew fond not only of her grandson but also of Maya who had a calm, peaceful air about her and could not be faulted in the care of her charge.

Maya felt comfortable around Tiya like she had around the Lady Kiya. The pace of life in this household was slower, free of the stress she experienced at Pharaoh's court.

Maya kept a close eye on Swnwt and whilst she could find no complaint with her work, she instinctively did not give Swnwt any duties which included bathing or feeding the growing infant. At six months breast milk had to be supplemented with porridge in the morning and at night.

It was some two hundred and seventy days since their arrival. Tiya and Maya were sitting in the shade of a large tree. Baby Tut was lying nearby, naked except for a fine linen vest, gurgling loudly to himself, chubby legs kicking. Maya looked at the woman beside her, petite yet strong and still attractive.

"Would you think me rude if I ask how you and your husband met?" she asked Tiya.

Tiya's almond eyes, bright with joy, said, "It would be a pleasure to tell you if you are really interested. I am the daughter of a nobleman. My father was a powerful military leader in his day. That is how Amenhotep and I met. We fell in love and, although there was resistance on his family's part since I was not of royal blood, he got his way. I learnt later that the palace spread word abroad that I was a Syrian Princess.

"We were married for years before he became Pharaoh, which I was grateful for because, by then, I was certain of his love for me. He consulted me on many matters of state and treated me as his equal in all aspects of royal life. He even had my statue at

Medinet Habu made to exactly the same dimensions as his own. Something that had never been done before in our history. Proof, if proof was needed, of his great love and regard for me. Now my dear, tell me something about yourself."

Maya smiled shyly, she had never had to recount her life to anyone before. Lady Kiya had known everything about her. She started hesitantly.

"I was left at the door of King Tushratta's palace orphanage when I was a few weeks old. At least so I was told. I was taken in and well looked after. Not much happened in my life until I was about nine. Princess Kiya wanted a playmate. I found out later she did not like any of the high- born children because, she said, *they were not in the least interesting.*" I had been learning to be a lady's maid and I knew how to play games with small stones and hide-and-seek but not much else. She visited the orphanage on her ninth birthday and chose me for a playmate.

"We became inseparable from that day. When she learnt of her proposed marriage to your son she told her father she would only accept if she could bring me with her. By this time we were both eighteen years old.

"Then it happened." Maya's face crumpled and a

dark cloud seemed to come over her.

"What is it, child?" asked Tiya. "Tell me, do."

Large tears rolled down Maya's face despite her best efforts. She wiped them away and composed herself.

"There was a nobleman at court who took a liking to me and would go out of his way to pay me compliments. He was a man in his prime, with a family so I thought he was being fatherly in giving me little presents but I was wrong.

"On the night of the banquet in honour of Princess Kiya's forthcoming nuptials, I was alone in my room awaiting her return. This man entered and before I could understand what was happening he deflowered me. While he was inside my body I felt an explosion. I don't know how else to explain it.

"After he left I struggled to sit up. There was sticky liquid oozing down my inner thighs. I noticed the sheet on my bed was soiled with blood. The lower part of me felt sore, and throbbed. Kiya found me in that condition when she came looking for me to tell me about the festivities."

"Did you tell her who the man was?" asked Tiya.

"I asked her what would happen to him if I revealed his identity to her. She said her father would have him flogged and possibly castrated. His lands and privileges would be taken from him."

"So what did you do?"

"I told Kiya I could not condemn his innocent wife and children to such disgrace. We were leaving the court soon to travel to Egypt so no one needed to know."

"Did Kiya agree to this?"

"Reluctantly, yes. Soon after we reached your son's court I discovered I was with child. Kiya told the Pharaoh that my husband had died fighting in her father's army.

"As the gods would have it, although I went full term, the child was born asleep. But now the gods have blessed me with another child, a prince no less, to love and care for."

"You are still young, my dear, surely you want to marry?"

"No thank you!" said Maya. "I don't ever want to experience again what I went through that night!"

"The sharing of bodies between two people who really love and care for each other is a beautiful, even delicious, experience."

"Well I have no desire or interest in that kind of love. Baby Tut is all I need."

This exchange of such intimate confidences brought the two women closer together and Maya found opportunity to seek answers to many questions concerning the customs and gods of Egypt. One morning when they were enjoying a walk round the flower gardens Maya asked Tiya to explain why it is Egyptians have no fear of death.

"Egyptians," explained Tiya, "are very close to nature. We have observed that the sun dies in the West each day only to rise again, to be reborn, in the East the next day. Take, for example, when one looks at a kernel of grain, it appears dead, yet when you put it in the ground it sprouts into new life.

"It is said the god Osiris was murdered by his envious brother Set who then chopped Osiris up and scattered his body over the length and breadth of Egypt. Osiris's wife Isis gathered all the parts together and, with the help of other gods, brought Osiris to life again. Thus the belief arose that since Osiris came back to life, others may also come back. Provided they prove worthy."

"How can they prove that?" asked Maya.

"You may not be aware of this custom," said Tiya, "but all the organs are taken from the body of the dead by the embalmers, except the heart. That is left in because it has to be weighed against the 'Feather of Truth'. Anubis, the god with the head of a dog and the body of a man, is the guardian of the dead.

"He holds the scales of justice. If the scales balance,

with the Feather on one side and the heart of the deceased on the other, it means that person has led a good life."

"And if it does not balance?" asked Maya.

"Then that person is thrown to a terrible monster called the Devourer. Sit down and I will explain the gods fully so you can teach the young Prince when the time comes.

"Amun is the god of Thebes. Re is the god of Heliopolis. Amun married Mut. They had two children Tefrut, meaning Moisture, and Shu, meaning Air.

"Tefrut and Shu are the parents of Geb, meaning Earth, and Nut, meaning Sky. Geb and Nut then had four children, Osiris, Isis, Set and Nephthys. Osiris and Isis had two children, Horus and Hathor. Set and Nephthys became god and goddess of Deserts and Storms.

"Isis is believed to be the loving mother of all and has more magical powers than any other god or goddess. Horus's right eye is the sun and his left eye, which was plucked out in battle, is the moon. He is usually depicted as a falcon. Hathor is the Queen of Heaven and the cow is her sacred animal. I will draw you a plan to make it easier for you to remember."

Maya looked uncomfortably at Tiya.

"Were you taught to read and write, Maya?" asked Tiya gently.

"No, only how to sew, wash and clean."

"Well, we will have to remedy that. Since you are as a mother to the future Pharaoh you must be able to assist him when he is old enough to learn."

So it was that Maya was schooled by the family scribe.

In time Tiya assisted Maya in understanding how the Government of Egypt operated. She explained that Pharaoh is the Head of Government. Below him is his Vizier and Second-in-Command. The Vizier runs the country by having regular meetings with the Chief Officers that make up the Internal Government.

"There are four branches; the Royal Domain, the Military, the Religious Representative and the Civil Section, with a leader for the North and another for the South territories.

"The Royal Domain is sub-divided into two parts; the Royal Court for which the Chancellor is responsible and the Estates for which the Chief Steward of the Royal Household is responsible.

"The Military is responsible for the commanders who are in turn responsible for the officer corps.

"The Religious section is also separated into two

parts consisting of the High Priest of Amun and the High Priests of the other gods and both are responsible for the lesser priesthood of which there are thousands.

"All those Chief Officers report to the Vizier who then keeps the Pharaoh informed.

"There are two areas within which the Pharaoh alone makes decisions after consultation with his Vizier and Advisers who are chosen from the most educated men in Egypt. The first relates to the Royal Family; the second to the Government of Conquests which consists of the Governor of the Northern Foreign Lands and the Governor of the Southern Foreign Lands. The Governors oversee the Vassal Kings, the Officer Corps, both North and South, as well as their own Deputies.

"Below this hierarchy is the Bureaucracy, made up of Scribes and below them are the *fellahin*, peasants. I have set it all out on this papyrus for you so you can show Tut when the time comes," concluded Tiya.

Before Maya knew it Prince Tut's first birthday arrived. He was a sturdy toddler, taking his first unsteady steps.

Nefertiti was pacing up and down her private room, wringing her hands and looking frustrated.

"Oh Poly! Where have you been? Has the girl made her report? What news of the Boy?"

Poly, a little alarmed at the state of her mistress, said soothingly, "Would you prefer to sit on the balcony and sip a glass of milk and honey?"

The Queen stared at her head housekeeper. "So the news is not good!"

"Swnwt reports the child is healthy and strong. Preparations are being made for celebrating his first birthday."

"I know that!" spat the Queen. "My beloved Akhenhaten has had his own man purchasing presents for the child."

The Queen's countenance cleared as an idea occurred to her.

"Poly, can you acquire a small wooden horse painted with poison mixed in with the paint? Make it bright red so it attracts the child's attention. They put everything in their mouths at that age. Have you someone you can trust to do this?"

"Highness, I can easily obtain a small, well carved wooden horse. I will mix the poison in the paint and colour the toy personally. My cousin, the palace's head housekeeper will arrange, discreetly, for the toy to be added to the bag of toys the King will be taking. Leave it to me."

Tiya was looking forward to her son's visit. She had the cook prepare all his favourite foods. She explained to Maya that he had not visited Thebes since the rift between father and son. She confessed to Maya that she missed her children so much it made her heart ache. Her older son died in his youth, she explained, and her four daughters were married and living outside Egypt with their own royal and family responsibilities.

Akhenaten, dressed as one of his soldiers, arrived at the agreed time with a small retinue. He greeted his mother cordially and, indeed, seemed pleased to see her. Maya had dressed Tut in a gold brocade outfit his grandmother had had made for his birthday.

She brought him into the main hall and put him down, encouraging him to walk to his grandmother who was standing near the King, arms outstretched. Tut, balancing himself with his arms raised on either side of his body, took his first proper steps. He got half way and fell on his bottom. The boy laughed as though he knew he had done well.

The King came forward and scooped him up. They had a long hard look at each other. Maya got the feeling father and son were deciding whether they liked each other. Tut then put his little chubby arms around his father's neck and snuggled into him.

Maya could swear there were tears in the King's eyes. She looked away so as not to cause any embarrassment. Tiya definitely had tears rolling down her cheeks.

In the main hall stood a long table laden with all manner of food and sweetmeats. Delicately flavoured kidneys which Tut loved mashed; pigeon stew; beef ribs cooked over an open fire; freshly made wheat bread, a variety of cheeses; salads and vegetables; small cakes, fresh dates, figs and berries. To drink there was wine, both grape and pomegranate, and beer brewed just the way Akhenaten liked it by Tiya's chief cook.

"Mother, there was no need to go to all this trouble. The child is only one year old. He will have no recollection of your efforts," said the King.

"It is not just for him, my son. I am so happy to see you sitting at my table."

The King smiled indulgently at his Mother. "It has been a long time since we have eaten together but I know you understand the reasons," said the King.

"Yes, my son. I do."

The King dined with his mother, Maya and Tut in her private quarters, while the King's retinue ate in the main hall. Akhenaten took the opportunity to ask after his father.

"Mother, I have tried to explain to father that the priests were a threat to the throne. I discovered they owned two thirds of all temple lands in Egypt and ninety per cent of her ships."

"I understand," said his mother. He took her hands in his and kissed each one in turn. It was his way of thanking her.

After the meal the King's servants brought in many gifts for Tut. The King, smiling indulgently, watched Tut playing with the small metal soldiers and a little horse painted bright red, the first gifts to catch the boy's attention, It did not take long for Tut to start chewing on the little red horse in his hand. Maya managed to take it off him and clean the paint off his hands and face as the King was saying goodbye to Tiya and then to his son.

Before leaving the King asked his Mother how Maya was developing. "I want to reward her for her faithful service."

His mother explained Maya was having lessons with the family scribe and learning about Egypt's history and customs.

"Good," he replied. "She will prove a good adviser to the young Prince."

That evening Tiya went to her husband's bed

chamber. He was sitting silently on a chaise near the open window. The night breeze wafted in imbued with the sweet scent of flowers from the garden below. She sat in the armchair opposite so she could see him clearly. He was looking old and sad.

"So, how was your son?" he asked after a few minutes silence.

"He enjoyed the food and was well pleased with the child's progress. He asked after you. Maya is doing a wonderful job of caring for the Prince and she is getting on well with her reading and writing. The scribe is impressed with her progress. I have been teaching her about our gods and how the government works."

"Our gods? Which ones?"

"Amun Re, naturally. I think you should start taking an interest in your grandson. You can teach him your views and principles so that when he is king he will want to bring back the old gods."

Amenhotep looked at his wife. "Now I remember why I married you," he said tenderly. "You have foresight."

Tiya smiled at him. "Would you like me to stay with you tonight" she asked shyly.

"I would like that very much," came the reply.

By midnight Tut was retching and his bowels were loose. The child was listless. He could not sit up. Nor could he hold down so much as a sip of water. Tiya sent for the family physician and despatched an urgent message, via one of the homing birds, to her son.

Maya racked her brains to think what may have caused the child to be ill. She had checked everything he ate and drank. Yet here he was in a cold sweat. She wiped him with a warm damp cloth and dried his body gently. She kept whispering his name but he did not respond. The doctor finally arrived. He examined the child and looked at the distressed women, shaking his head.

"The child is displaying all the signs of poisoning yet you say he ate nothing different from the two of you?"

"Yes," came the reply. It was in an instant that Maya remembered taking the red horse away from Tut. She looked at the doctor, explained her thoughts and ran to retrieve the soldiers and horse from the toy box. The doctor sniffed the items handed to him.

"The horse smells odd. I will take this away and check the paint and wood and will send a report to the King and to you, Lady Tiya. In the meantime feed the young Prince small spoonfuls of plain chicken broth. I will be back in a few hours to check on him and may need to stay with him."

"I will see to the arrangements," said Lady Tiya. Maya was in a daze. Surely the King would have used his most trusted servants to procure the presents for his son. How could the poisoned item have found its way into the King's inner- most sanctum? She did not leave Tut's side unless the Lady Tiya was with him. Swnwt and Zelda did what was needed and brought fresh broth and water which Maya tasted before offering the Prince.

Swnwt asked permission to send a message by dove to her mother which Tiya granted without any enquiry as to why. The message stated the Prince was seriously ill from an unknown ailment.

Later that day the doctor confirmed the paint on the horse contained a deadly poison. He could not be certain whether it was cobra or scorpion's venom.

"From the little teeth marks on the toy it appears the Prince absorbed enough of the poison to make him poorly but not to kill him. That is my hope based on the fact that the Prince is looking brighter. No more cold sweats, at least."

In the early hours of the following morning the King

arrived with the royal physician, Ir-En-Okhty who examined the child, had a discussion with the family doctor and turned to the King, handing him the painted horse, wrapped in papyrus for safety.

"This is the weapon used to harm the child. The wet-nurse says it was among the toys given to the Prince on his birthday."

The King looked at the toy and at the listless child who was attempting to smile at him. He then looked at Maya, standing on the other side of the bed close by Tut. "Had you not been quick to take the toy from my son, he could be dead now. This is the second time you have saved him. His mother chose well."

The King kissed his son on the forehead and left the room.

"Mother, the toy soldiers and horses I brought are all made of metal. This is made of wood and is not something I commissioned." As though speaking to himself he continued "What is the best way of dealing with this act of treason? Say nothing and be vigilant, or investigate and risk word spreading abroad that an attempt has been made on the Prince's life?"

His mother looked at him with sombre eyes. "You will make the right decision. For myself I would prefer it not to be known. We can, if asked, explain the bout as an infant's ailment."

It was ten days before Tut returned to his usual lively self. His appetite returned and so did the strength in his limbs. His grandfather had visiting him when he was ill and his visits continued as Tut's strength returned.

Swnwt was closely questioned by Poly when she next visited her mother but since the poisoned toy was a closely guarded secret she had no knowledge of it and could only state the child had been ill but was now well again. Since there had been no investigation neither Poly nor the Queen could be sure whether the poisoned toy was the cause of the illness.

Chapter 5

Amenhotep, Tut's grandfather, visited Tut for a short time each day while the child was ill. This continued after Tut regained his strength. Sometimes they met in the garden or when Tut was playing indoors with the toys his father had given him for his birthday. Before long the time they spent together stretched to half an hour; then to an hour and gradually grandfather and grandson were firm friends. Amenhotep could not believe the joy he derived from spending time with his grandson.

By the age of three Tut was speaking in proper sentences, had a good vocabulary and a highly-developed sense of humour for one so young. Some may even say he was precocious. He was always surprising his *Gidu*, grandfather, with his antics. Tut would hide items belonging to his Gidu in the most unlikely places and would only produce them when Gidu gave up trying to find them. One day he hid his Gidu's favourite hunting knife, with the jewel encrusted handle, in the linen box. His grandfather was in the room the whole time yet did not see the child go near the linen box.

Amenhotep decided the time was right to speak to Tut about changes that would be needed when Tut was Pharaoh. He realised time was not on his side.

Lately he had had a foreboding of his own demise. When Maya next brought Tut to his grandfather the two walked in the flower garden and along the avenue of trees where seats were provided, at regular intervals, so the old and the very young could rest.

"What are you thinking about grandfather?"

"Oh, call me Gidu, Tut, it makes me happy. I must be getting old! Let us sit here a while. You remember we have talked about the gods of Egypt?"

"Yes, you have explained the changes Father made to the religion of the country since taking the throne."

"I can never forgive my son for his betrayal in outlawing the worship of Amun. He closed all the temples and confiscated their lands and goods. This, to me, is blasphemy.

"This heretic child of mine then set himself up as High Priest of his new religion and declared there was no need for priests since he could speak direct to the Aten."

"What is the religion of Aten, Gidu?"

"Your father claims it is the worship of the sun which he shows as a solar disc whose life giving rays terminate in hands holding the ankh, the symbol of life. He has gone further and built a temple to the impostor immediately outside the East Gate of Amun's temple at Karnak."

"I do not understand everything you just said, Gidu, but I can see you feel very strongly about Amun."

His grandfather looked at Tut, his face losing its scowl. "It is asking a great deal of a three-year- old but when you are Pharaoh will you promise me you will reinstate the Amun religion?"

"Do you mean open Karnak temple and give the lands, ships and treasurers back to the priests of Amun?"

"That is exactly what I mean. Will you promise me that, Tut?"

"Yes, Gidu, I promise."

"And you will not forget your Gidu and your promise when you get older, will you?"

"No! I could never forget you as long as I live."

"You have made an old man very happy. Come, let us continue our walk."

Maya was a little way off keeping an eye on the two men of the household. She could see the old king was getting weary and wanted to be on hand in case he needed assistance.

That afternoon while Maya was teaching Tut his letters, he seemed deep in thought and not his usual attentive self.

"Maya, you are not going to die and leave me are

you?"

"Certainly not. Why do you ask such a question?"

"Well, my mother died and left me and I think Gidu and Nana will do the same. I could not bear for you to leave me too." He bravely fought back tears.

"You are very serious for a boy of three," said Maya, laughing, trying to lighten his mood.

"Maya, you, Gidu and Nana have taught me I am no ordinary boy. I will be King one day. I have so much to learn, so much to understand. The sooner I grow up the better for my country."

"Well you have a few years yet. Let's leave this lesson for a while and play hide-and-seek. I will count to ten and then come looking for you but you must stay within our part of the palace."

Tut smiled, nodded his head in agreement and scooted off. Maya heaved a heartfelt sigh. Time enough for such weighty thoughts.

That night before retiring to bed the old King retrieved from his scroll library the papyrus on which was written a poem by Vizier Ptahotep. He felt the need to read it again.

"Age is here, old age arrived.
Feebleness come, weakness grows.
Childlike one sleeps all day,

Eyes are dim, ears deaf,
Strength is waning through weariness,
The mouth silenced, speaks not the past
The bones ache throughout
Good has become evil, all taste is gone,
What age does to people is evil in every way."

He smiled ruefully to himself remembering the
Coffin Text which states,
"He who understands life will live to be a hundred
and ten."

Amenhotep understood life as much as any man of
learning yet felt sure he would not live to such a great
age. With that thought he climbed into his inviting,
comfortable bed.

Chapter 6

It was the season of Peret, the sprouting season, in the month of Renwet, when the old king slipped peacefully away in his sleep.

Tiya, waking up earlier than usual, decided to surprise her husband by taking breakfast with him as they used to do when they were first married.

She walked quietly into his bedchamber and climbed into bed beside him, putting her cheek against his. She was surprised that it felt cold. She looked up to see whether the windows were open. No, the shutters were closed. She looked at her husband again. He was strangely still. She put her ear to his heart but could not hear the familiar thud, thud sound that usually told her all was well in her world.

The truth dawned on her although every fibre of her body fought against believing it. She got off the bed, hurried to the servants' quarters and sent her head gardener, who was already up and dressed, to bring the doctor. She made it clear to him she did not want the servants alarmed.

Tiya then went to Maya's room. She also was up and ready for the day. Thankfully Tut was still asleep. Tiya beckoned Maya to follow her. Maya alerted Swnwt to watch Tut. The two women walked silently to Amenhotep's bed chamber. Maya realised immediately they entered the room that the old king had passed on. Without thinking she hugged Tiya who did not react other than to inform Maya that the doctor had been sent for. Maya moved the arm chair close to the bed and put Tiya to sit down. She poured a glass of pomegranate wine and put it in Tiya's hand with firm instruction to drink all of it.

She then ensured all was in order in the room. She called the old king's personal body servant, informing him of his master's demise, asking him to keep it to himself for the time being and to clean the toilet, putting fresh sand in the bucket.

The family physician arrived and confirmed the old king was no more. Still Tiya was dry-eyed. She instructed Maya to get a message to the Pharaoh since it was his responsibility, being the only son alive, to see to his father's burial. Tiya stated she would write to her four daughters.

"They are unlikely to attend their father's funeral. He and I were always away when they were growing and we are strangers, in some ways, to our children. So my older daughter informed me when she married, vowing to be a better mother to her children," she said to Maya.

Having ensured Tut was taken care of, Maya, with the doctor's assistance, arranged for the embalmers to take the body. The doctor then took his leave.

"Tiya, how is it you are dry-eyed?" asked Maya.

"The sadness of death is felt by the living because they have to do without the deceased. Having lived a good, full and useful life, my husband has experienced the best death possible. No illness or pain, he just slipped away in sleep. I could ask no more for him. We shared a passionate love for each other which grew deeper with the years. He will reside with the gods when all the rituals are completed. What need is there for tears when we will be together again in the afterlife?"

It was two days before the Pharaoh arrived. He greeted his mother with more emotion than he had displayed since a child. He put his arms around her and held her close to his chest, almost as though he wanted to protect her from the pain of her loss. She led him to his father's chambers.

"Mother, we have seventy days to provide for Father's needs in the next world. I will give instructions for seeds, food and treasured possessions to be placed in the tomb. Can you provide the personal things he would want with him?"

His mother inclined her head in the affirmative. "I will arrange refreshments for you and your guards," she said as she left the room.

Akhenaten went through his father's papers to ascertain his burial wishes. He sent a message to the Head Embalmer, Merenuka, instructing him to ensure all funeral rites, according to the God Amun, were strictly followed and confirming the various canopic jars for his father's internal organs would be sent shortly. He then joined his mother for a late lunch.

"Mother I am preparing a villa for you, Tut and both households' servants at the new capital. The villa will be on the other side of the town from the Palace so that Tut can continue to enjoy your companionship and the peace and tranquility that affords."

"I am so happy to hear you say that. I thought you might want him at the Palace. I could not bear, at this time, to lose either Tut or Maya. They have both become very precious to me."

"I will send word when the villa is ready. It is not likely to be before Father has been entombed. I have to return to the capital but will send trusted servants to take what is needed to Father's tomb. Stay well Mother," said the King, kissing her hands as he took his leave.

Before long word spread of Amenhotep III demise and messages of respect for the Great Memnon flooded in from Libya, Nubia, Palestine, Syria and the Asiatic. Presents were received to accompany the old king on his journey to Osiris.

Tut did not at first understand why he could not have his usual daily walk with his Gidu. Maya took him to the garden and explained that his grandfather was now with the gods, he was happy and Tut would see him again when he became an old man and passed away.

"So you see, there is no need to be sad." said Maya.

"But I am sad," said Tut, "because I will miss him and our talks."

"Do you remember what you talked about?"

"Of course I do."

"So long as you remember, your Gidu will remain alive in here," she said, pointing to his heart, "and here," pointing to his head. "As long as you are alive, he is alive."

Tut sensed his Nana needed him. She did not speak much to anyone and would sit in her private quarters or in the garden with a faraway look on her face. He stayed close to her every opportunity he got. When in the garden he sat beside her, looking at the water of the dancing fountain catching the sunlight and sparkling like tiny jewels, wondering where his Gidu was now.

Chapter 7

Maya kept Tut busy with learning his letters, reading and running around the garden playing hide and seek with Swnwt, whom Maya had come to trust over the years. Swnwt acquired some pieces of pottery from the family Scribe and Maya gave her a palate and colours Tut had been given for his third birthday. Tut loved painting with the bright colours. Swnwt thus kept the young Prince entertained when Maya was needed to assist Tiya.

Swnwt had grown into a very attractive young woman, with long lashed almond eyes, cherry red lips and thick wavy dark hair and lithe body. She had become devoted to Tut. She prayed every day that she would not receive instructions to do anything to harm the child. To date her prayers had been answered. Swnwt had made her usual monthly report to Polydama when Swnwt visited her mother at the Palace. This she usually did on the last day of each month, that being her free day. She had heard rumours that the household would be moving to the capital and hoped she would be able to remain with Tut's household. The work was easy, the food and accommodation good; everything was better than she could have hoped for.

Swnwt recollected the strange eerie feeling she use

to get when close to Tut, as though she was being watched, even when she knew it could not be Maya. She shuddered at the recollection. Thank goodness she had not experienced that feeling for a while now.

"Look at this Swnwt," said Tut, whose fingers were covered in paint. Red, blue, yellow, green and orange stripes were on the pottery. "It looks like the painting in the sky when the rains come," he said.

"You are right! You have done really well. Such good control of the brush," said Swnwt. He looked at her and smiled.

"I like painting. Can we do it again?"

"Of course, if Maya says you can. Next time I can explain to you the meaning of the colours. Would you like that?" Tut nodded that he would.

Nefertiti had received Swnwt's monthly report on the Prince's progress and was not impressed that, apart from his illness following his first birthday, he had not contracted any of the usual childhood diseases. The fact that he did not mix with other children his own age probably accounted for his unusual good health.

She gave serious consideration to sending a potion to Swnwt to put in the child's drink but decided against it. There was no guarantee the girl would not give them away.

Her husband was mourning the loss of his father and would not come to her bed until after the final burial ceremony. He confided in her that whilst he did not regret his action in changing the religion, he regretted the rift it caused between himself and his father.

"He was a great leader, Nef. He was not around much when I was growing up but he made Egypt the rich nation she is today by his successful campaigns and by shrewdly marrying my sisters to leaders strategic to protecting Egypt's borders thus binding their countries to ours."

There is still another three years to go, anything could still happen, thought the Queen as she comforted her husband.

Lady Tiya wondered at her son instructing rather than discussing with her the move to the new capital after his father's death. She would have preferred to have been consulted. After all it is what her husband had always done before making a decision which directly affected her. How times have changed, she thought.

When they moved to the Small Palace she was involved in discussions with the architect, the decorators, the tradespeople, in fact with everyone involved.

Now she had no idea what to expect. She had had

all the wall hangings and paintings taken down and packed. Also the ornaments she had collected or been given over the years: beautifully carved ivory animals; ebony carved elephants and giraffes from Africa and Nubia; sandalwood carved gods from the Indus; combs and items of jewellery. Her gold and bejewelled pieces had already been shared between her daughters. She had given each one a part share on their getting married. One less matter to concern herself with.

On the last night in the home she had occupied with her beloved for some fifteen years, she wandered around her favourite rooms, visiting her husband's quarters last, caressing the chair he use to sit in, opening the drawers and touching the few items not put into the tomb with him.

She laid her head on the bed where he last laid his head and breathed in deeply as thought trying to capture and keep close the scent of him.

How quickly the years have flown, she thought. She returned to her quarters and lay in bed listening, for the last time, to the familiar noises: the footsteps of the guards marching round the grounds, speaking occasionally in hushed tones; the birds settling down for the night; the distant lapping of water against the Nile bank. Lady Tiya slowly drifted off to sleep.

The move from Thebes to Akhenhaten was arduous. The new Capital was situated about half way between Thebes and Memphis. The way was dry, hot and uncomfortable. There were more soldiers guarding the travellers on this journey.

Maya noticed the young man Nakhtmia she had seen three years earlier. He appeared to be about eighteen years old. Her heart skipped a beat. He had matured. His shoulders had broadened, his waist was more defined. His white kilt rested easily on his hips. His thighs were muscular and shone in the morning light. He waved to her as their eyes met. She withdrew her head hurriedly, feeling hot all over her body. She could not explain, even to herself, why or how this young man managed to take her breath away.

It was difficult, on this occasion, to keep Tut occupied. He kept hanging out of the carriage openings, wanting to sit with the driver. Both Swnwt and Zelda were in the carriage with Maya. The Lady Tiya was in her own coach with her aged handmaiden, Edfu. When they stopped to rest the animals and have something to eat Maya took Tut behind a sand dune to relieve himself.

Soldiers were milling around, keeping a watchful eye

on the Prince. As Maya and Tut were about to walk back to the coach Maya was knocked to the ground. She felt a heavy weight on her. She started to scream but a rough, dirty hand covered her mouth. She thought she was going to be raped again. She was so angry at the thought she managed to sink her teeth into the hand over her mouth. As the hand was pulled away she let out a piercing scream. The next thing she knew she was being helped up. She looked round frantically.

"Where is the Prince?" she cried.

The young man she had recognised earlier had his arm around her steadying her. "He too was attacked but he is only bruised and shaken."

It was then Maya noticed a man, with the build of a soldier, sprawled on his back, his throat cut. She looked questioningly at the young soldier. "Is this your work, Nakhtmia?"

"You remembered my name," he said, sounding pleased. "I had no choice. He was about to despatch the Prince. Look at the dagger still clasped in his hand!"

"Could you not have disabled him so that he could be questioned?"

Nakhtmia looked crestfallen. "I reacted according to my training but I see your point. I should have thought."

"There was another man. I bit his hand," explained Maya.

"I saw no-one."

"Where could he be hiding? If only we could find him. He was broad and heavy. He knocked me down from behind, I just felt his heavy body on me and he smelt of horses. Get the soldiers to make a thorough search."

Nakhtmia bowed slightly and went to speak to Tiya's Captain.

Maya made her way back to the coach. Her body felt bruised and painful. Tut was sitting quietly on Swnwt's lap. As soon as he saw Maya his eyes welled up.

"Maya, why would anyone want to kill me? What have I done wrong? She took him in her arms and held him close.

"You have done nothing wrong. There are some people, we do not know who, that do not want you to become Pharaoh."

"Why not? I will be a good Ruler, like my Gidu."

"I have no answer for you. Let me see you eat and drink something then I must let your Nana know all is well with you."

Nakhtmia, having instigated a search, had returned

to Maya and was standing beside the open coach. She jumped as she heard him say, "The Captain has informed the Lady Tiya of the situation."

"Please escort us to her coach. We will travel with her for the rest of the way."

Maya and Tiya examined Tut's body after they had had some refreshment. There was bruising on his upper arms and neck but nothing seemed to be broken. He lay down for his afternoon nap without complaint as they continued their journey.

As the last cart disappeared from the scene of the attack no one noticed a movement in the sand. Nor did they see a large man shaking sand off himself while nursing his hand staring at the carts in the distance.

"Tiya, how are we to protect Tut if his enemies are not put off by soldiers guarding him?" asked Maya.

"The King will find a way to keep his son safe. I recollect him telling me there is a high wall surrounding the villa, with sturdy gates manned by a retired soldier."

There had been no opportunity for the women to visit the property before the move. However, the King had sent his mother a plan of the house and land. Decisions on what furniture and furnishings were needed and allocation of quarters were yet to be made. To be safe Tiya travelled with everything she thought they might require.

Maya had been told by Tiya that their villa consisted of about twenty rooms. There was a suite for Tiya and her handmaiden, Edfu, on the ground floor together with guests quarters; the same for Tut's household on the first floor.

"The servants," she said, "were being housed in a building adjoining the villa."

Before the move Tiya, who loved her gardens, had long meetings with her head gardener, Manetho, a strapping man in his prime with a head of thick dark hair; a handsome if weather- beaten face and large capable hands.

They agreed on which plants, flowering bushes and trees could be dug up and successfully replanted in the new garden and, relying on the plan provided, where the various trees could best be located.

All Tiya's servants had agreed to accompany her to her new home, although she had had to let some under-gardeners go since not all would be needed at the villa. With the help of her head gardener she managed to find them work in the homes of retired dignitaries in the surrounding area.

As they approached the Capital Tiya explained to

Maya and Tut that she understood, from her talk with Akhenaten, that the city stretched along the Nile with their villa located on the side of the town away from the river.

When they travelled through the town Tiya pointed out her son's town residence and facing it, on the other side, joined by an overhead bridge spanning the busy thoroughfare, was the Government Palace where meetings were held and scribes worked.

"The Royal Palace," explained Tiya, "is on the bank of the Nile along the northern rim of the city."

Maya listened attentively since, she thought, she would need to find her way around the city in order to ensure she was able to guide and teach Tut as he grew. As they approached the villa, huge, ornate wooden gates swung open to allow them in. The gate keeper bowed and introduced himself to Tiya. An extensive but sparsely planted garden spread out on either side of the path leading to the villa.

On seeing that the land within the walls was bare of trees or plants, Tiya felt pleased she had brought much of what had been in her old garden. She made a mental note to instruct Manetho to plant some fruit trees for Tut to enjoy. Some pomegranate, figs and date palms would go well over there to the right of the path, she thought.

At the end of the path, raised on a plinth, stood the villa, reached by ascending two deep steps. There were ornate bars on either side of the steps to assist Tiya's access into the building should she need help as she got older. Very thoughtful of the Pharaoh's Architect, thought Tiya as she made her way into her new home. So this is where I shall die after a life of opulence and plenty. My compensation is Tut and Maya. I have no regrets.

To the right of the entrance was a hall leading to the servants' quarters and the outdoor covered kitchen area. Maya and Tut explored while Tiya sat in the cool reception area enjoying a glass of juice. Tut appeared to have forgotten the attack on his life.

The resilience of children, marvelled Tiya as she watched him scamper off."

They came back and reported to her that there were many storerooms for food, washing, making of bread and beer and for storage of garden tools at the rear of the servants' quarters. Indoors, all the rooms had basic furniture, beds, chests for clothes, bedding and towels. Every apartment, they reported, had ample bath and toilet facilities.

Since it was getting late and everyone was tired Maya promised Tut they would explore further the next day. A wash to get the dust of the journey off, something to eat and bed was what was needed.

Maya explained to Tiya's housekeeper the sleeping arrangements for Tut and Maya, for Tiya and her ageing maid as well as for Tut's handmaidens, and asked that the beds be made and warm water be put in the bathrooms before providing a simple supper of bread and honey with warm milk for Tiya and Tut.

One of the maids reported a shortage of lamps. Maya gave instructions for those in the carts to be brought in and prepared so they could be lit since the sun was about to set. There was much activity as some servants brought linen and others clothes boxes into the villa whilst others were taking food and utensils into the servants' quarters.

Just as the household was having a light supper, a courtier arrived accompanied by a cartload of fresh produce from the Palace gardens and a message from the King.

He apologised for not being there to greet his mother and asked her to send him a note, with the same messenger, as to what assistance might be needed to make her comfortable in her new home.

Since Tiya had only seen the garden area she asked for assistance with preparing the garden for trees, a small pond and a fountain. She stated she would consult her head gardener and housekeeper to see what else might be needed and would let the King know.

That night, although exhausted and aching all over, Tiya could not sleep. There was no reminder of her beloved Amen in this building. She could no longer wander into his room and lose herself in the smell of him, the feel of his presence all around her.

Maybe it is for the best, she thought to herself. Life is for the living. I will be with the dead soon enough, she decided.

That evening at the Palace the Captain of the Elite Guard reported the attack to the King as it was told to him by his soldiers that were on that detail.

"We need to take one of these criminals alive," said the King. "Put together a group of our best retired but still fit soldiers to keep watch day and night over the Prince. They must see without being seen. I have no doubt they will try again. Keep me informed."

The Captain bowed and left.

Over the next couple of days Maya discovered a well-finished and spacious roof.
This will be wonderful for studying the stars at night with Tut, she thought.

She and Tut wandered around the large open space at the front of the villa. There were no seats or shade in the front garden and they both agreed it could do with a water feature to help them feel cool. There was also a large piece of land at the rear for a vegetable garden.

Maya discussed the work needed in the front with Tiya and suggested it be started soon since Tut's fourth birthday was only sixty days away. Tiya involved Maya and Tut in the meeting with Manetho regarding the setting out of the garden. Manetho had drawn a plan and marked on it where Tiya wanted her flower garden to be as well as where Tut and Maya wanted the water feature and shaded seats and tables.

"Can we have fishes in the pond, Nana?" asked Tut.

Tiya looked at her gardener.

"That should not be a problem, Highness," replied Manetho.

There was then a general discussion about the fruit and other trees.

"Manetho, I will leave it to you to decide what to plant in the vegetable garden. No doubt you will consult the cooks. The King will be sending you some labourers to prepare the ground for planting."

Chapter 8

By the time Tut's birthday came around the garden and villa looked and felt as though the family had been living there for years. The trees were planted and flourishing in the well irrigated soil; the pond had fishes swimming around and hiding under the Nile lilies, reminding Tut of the Small Palace. The spouting water fountain in the centre of the pond cooled the air around.

The King was accompanied by his two younger daughters. One appeared to be about thirteen years old and the other, rather shy, looked about ten years old. Tut took an immediate liking to the ten year old and straight away took her by the hand to show her the fishes. He paid no attention to either his father or the presents he had brought. Maya took these to Tut's room and later reminded Tut to thank his father.

Maya and Tiya tried to have a conversation with the older girl but she was sullen and uncommunicative. When Tiya went for a walk with her son before lunch, Maya took the older girl to have a look round the villa, for want of something to do with her.

"How is your mother and other sisters?" asked Maya in all innocence.

"Why do you want to know?" spat the younger

woman.

Maya was taken aback. She had clearly grown out of the habit of considering palace intrigue.

"I am sorry, I was just making conversation. Are you not pleased to visit your grandmother?"

"I have never met her before today. I know nothing about her except that she is my father's parent.

"She is a worldly wise woman and worth becoming acquainted with. She tells wonderful stories of when your grandfather was Pharaoh."

The girl looked at Maya but said nothing. Maya found Swnwt and asked her to stay close to the Princesses in case they needed anything.

Lunch was enjoyed by everyone. There was freshly made sesame seed bread; freshly chopped onions, crushed garlic paste, various dips and chutneys made from vegetables from the King's garden; green salads; roasted ducks, pigeons and a suckling pig.

Fresh fruits, dates, figs and small cinnamon cakes washed down with pomegranate juice for the younger ones and Maya who liked neither wine or beer, beer for the King and grape wine for Tiya. Tut sat beside his new friend. It was not until the King and his retinue had left that it dawned on Tut that he had not asked his new friend her name.

Tiya went for a rest while Maya took Tut to his room for a wash and bed.

"Maya, can I open some of my presents first?" he asked.

She managed to coax him to wash first. She realised he was becoming more assertive. He was certainly growing up. His father had brought him many parcels. There was a small bow made from imported wood inscribed with Tut's throne name together with arrows made entirely of wood with a feather on the end of each. Tut fell in love with the brightly coloured feathers. When he eventually examined the other end of the arrows, he found the tips were also of wood, crafted to a sharp point.

There was a boomerang, the curved type which returned to the thrower. There were also an assortment of colourful cloaks and pharaonic headdresses with lapis lazuli clasps, summer shirts and kilts with clasps at the waist and several pairs of leather footwear of colours matching the cloaks.

"Maya, can we go hunting birds by the Nile? I want to try out my bow and arrow."

"You need to learn how to use it first," said Maya, "and then I promise to take you."

"Who will teach me?"

"I will talk to your Nana and see what can be

done. Now, bed. You have had a busy day."

"Maya, tell me again about my mother."

"She was a beautiful princess, daughter of King Tushratta. She was sent to Egypt to marry the Pharaoh in order to secure peace between the two countries and I came with her as her companion and handmaiden."

That night Tut had a vivid dream such as he had never had before.

He dreamt his mother was sitting beside his bed, smiling at him and tenderly caressing his hair.

"Hello, my son," she whispered. "You don't know me but I have been watching over you from the moment you were born. You had a lovely birthday celebration. Sleep, my baby." She kissed him on both cheeks and then just faded away. This was how Tut described his dream to Maya the next day.

"How did the dream make you feel, happy or sad?" asked Maya.

"I felt very happy," said Tut.

"Then it was a good dream."

Tiya decided to remain in her room the following day. She was feeling sad that she had not been able to engage in conversation with her granddaughters. Granted it was their first meeting. What was clear and shocking to her was the fact that neither girl seemed to know anything about her, their own grandmother. She decided both parents must have been too busy to acquaint their children with the filial connection. Tiya waited for an opportunity to suggest to her son her visiting the palace to meet all her granddaughters.

Chapter 9

Tiya consulted her son concerning Tut being taught to use his bow and arrow. This led to a young man turning up at the villa some days later. He stated to Tiya that he was from the Army training school and had been asked by his uncle, the Vizier, to teach the young Prince the art of shooting.

The young man appeared to be about eighteen years of age and introduced himself as Nakhtmia, a soldier nearing the end of his training. He had his bow and arrows slung across his shoulder and held a wooden board with circles painted on it.

"You have come prepared to start your duties, I see," said Tiya.

"I had hoped to commence lessons today unless it is inconvenient."

"No. The Prince is eager to start." Tiya hit a small gong standing on the table beside her chaise and a maid appeared.

"Ask Maya to come to me and bring the Prince with her." Holding her hand up to keep the servant for a moment Tiya turned to Nakhtmia. "Would you care for some refreshment, perhaps a glass of pomegranate juice?" He nodded his thanks.

"That is kind of you."

Tiya turned to the servant and inclined her head.

The servant bowed and left, and before long she returned with an earthenware jug of cool drink and four glasses. Maya and Tut followed a few minutes later.

Tiya introduced Tut and Maya to Nakhtmia and explained Nakhtmia was sent to teach Tut how to use his bow and arrows. Nakhtmia, who seemed unable to take his eyes off Maya, turned to the Lady Tiya.

"My Lady, I have met the Prince and Maya on two previous occasions. The first was when they travelled to your home in Thebes from the Royal Palace and the second when you all travelled from Thebes to this villa.

"On both occasions I was impressed by Maya's instinctive bravery and dedication to her charge." Maya felt her face getting hot as Tut looked at her and then at Nakhtmia.

"You have met me before? How is it I do not remember you?" asked Tut.

"On the first occasion you were a babe in arms and on the second, not many moons ago, you had been attacked and, I suspect, in shock."

Tut thought hard for a while and then asked,

"Were you the one with the bright feather on your head?"

"That was me."

Tut asked Nakhtmia to wait a moment. He ran out of the room and came rushing back, breathless, as Nakhtmia was sipping his drink, Tut showed the young man his bow and arrows.

"My father gave me this for my birthday. I am four now," he said with pride. "Can I call you Nakht? You can call me Prince if you like."

The two seemed to take to each other. Maya, trying not to show the confusing emotions she was feeling at the sight of Nakht, accompanied Tut and Nakht to the front, away from the busy gardeners. The target was set up and Nakht showed Tut how to hold the bow, position the arrow, line up the target and shoot.

At the end of the lesson Nakht promised to return at the same time the following week. He asked Maya whether she would walk with him to the gate. Maya looked at Tiya who indicated her consent.

"Tut and I will wait here for you," she said.

As they walked together to the rear of the garden to Nakht's horse Maya felt shy and at a loss for words. Nakht gave her a sidelong glance.

"You are more beautiful than when we first met. You have bloomed in the last four years. I have thought about you many times but had not the confidence to try and see you. Destiny has brought us together. I believe we are meant to be friends."

As Nakht untied his horse, Maya looked at his chiselled features, his dark mischievous eyes, the long, thick lashes, the generous, inviting mouth and sighed deeply.

"I have no objection to being friends so long as it is understood I live for the Prince. He is the first and only love in my life."

Nakht's eyes glowed with a hint of sadness. I admire your loyalty and would expect no less of you. Have you had nightmares about your first kill?"

"You say that as though killing is a sport to be relished. Yes, I did for many weeks. The act of taking a life haunted me but I eased my conscience with the fact that it was him or Tut and my duty is to Tut at all costs. I would do it again if I had to."

"I do not consider killing a sport." A pained look flitted across his face. "As a soldier I am aware the first time one kills is the worst. It gets easier after that. Killing is part of the trade of being a soldier. Like you, I would prefer that it were not so but my love for Egypt eases my burden of guilt at ending a life."

He spoke with such feeling that Maya felt sorry for her outburst. "Forgive me. I am untutored in the ways of the world," she said.

"That is why you intrigue me so," he said as he mounted his horse and galloped away, turning back to wave at her, a big smile on his young, handsome face.

Tut learned quickly and not many moons had passed before Maya thought it safe to take Tut shooting along the Nile.

She asked Nakht whether, in the interest of Tut's safety, he would accompany them. He readily agreed. She had come to think of him as a very pleasant, capable, young man who, Maya secretly admitted to herself, made her weak at the knees. A sensation she had never experienced before and was at pains to hide from him.

On the day of the outing Nakht arrived early as had been agreed, before the sun became too hot. Maya had a leather bag with water, dates and some nuts.
The sky was azure blue and the air balmy. Tut, with bow and arrows in a leather pouch on his shoulder, was skipping alongside Nakht.

Maya, who was walking behind the two young men, noted Nakht wore nothing but a short kilt tied low on the waist. Across his golden brown shoulders was a leather bag with his arrows. She felt shivers run up and down her spine which she tried to ignore.

"This is another new feeling," said she to her inner self. "Are you lingering back here just to gawp at that manly figure of rude good health and youthful vigour?" She vehemently denied the accusation to herself but had to bite her lower lip to stop herself smiling.

As they came in sight of the Nile, Tut stopped abruptly. He was mesmerised. Maya realised the child had not seen the river before. He took a deep breath and pulled himself up to his full height, walked to the water's edge, bent down, scooped some water in his hands, touched it to his lips and then splashed his face with what was left. Nakht and Maya looked at each other. Maya shrugged her shoulders.

"Are you thirsty, Tut?" she asked.

"The Nile water is sweet. I just wanted to taste it," he replied.

In the distance was a lone fishing boat, the fisherman busy casting his net. On the far bank the date palm trees were still. Under them *fellahin* women and servants, some wrapped in brightly-coloured cloth, were fetching water in large pitchers which they then carried on their head. On the near side, the reeds were noisy with water fowls, ducks and birds all looking for a meal with which to break their night fast.

"This is a good place to put your shooting practice to use," said Nakht to Tut. Tut beckoned to Maya and handed her his arrow pouch to hold for him.

"Can we find a clearing for me to sit before you two wander off" she asked.

Having found Maya a shaded area from where she could see them, the two went in search of water birds. Nakht indicated to Tut to be quiet so as not to frighten away the game. Tut had plenty of practice but did not in fact manage to kill any birds. Nakht had to retrieve several of Tut's arrows from among the reeds. Tut managed to find some colourful feathers which he brought to show Maya.

They had a drink and ate a few dates stuffed with nuts in place of the date seed. Tut, without saying anything, took out from his leather holder a small knife with an ornate jewel-encrusted handle that his father had given him for his third birthday and wandered over to the reeds. He leaned forward to get hold of the reed he had his eye on and before Maya realised he was not still beside her, Tut fell forward into the river.

The splash brought both Maya and Nakht running. Maya, distraught, shouted to Nakht that Tut could not swim. Nakht jumped into the water as Tut was coming up for the second time, got hold of the boy and brought them safely to the bank. As he did so Nakht noticed, from the corner of his eye, a young Nile crocodile swimming purposefully towards him.

He scrambled out of the water as the creature submerged, to get its prey by the leg, only just missing its target. Although out of breath Tut seemed unharmed.

"Maya, I was not afraid, I felt as though something was holding me up. No water went up my nose even when my head went under."

Maya's face was a picture of misery which caused Nakht to decide to say nothing of the presence of the crocodile.

"If you had been injured, I would have died," she said hugging Tut close. Tut was surprised at the depth of emotion he felt emanating from Maya. If Maya, usually calm and in control, was so upset, how would his Nana feel when told?

"Maya, please promise me you will not say anything of this to my grandmother. She may stop me coming to the river and I could not bear that. I want to come here again and again until I can kill a bird with my bow and arrow. And look, I kept hold of my knife." Turning to Nakht he asked, "Will you teach me to swim when we come to the river again? Will you also promise to tell no-one of this mishap?"

They both promised.

"Sorry Maya," said Nakht. "I was busy sorting my bow and arrows to put away."

"I cannot recollect what I was doing," she replied.

"Day-dreaming no doubt."

"About me?" asked Nakht. They both laughed.

"That's better," he said.

They remained by the river until Tut and Nakht were dry, which did not take long. They then wandered back to the villa where Nakht joined them for lunch.

Tut showed his Nana the feathers he had found and told her he would wear them in his hair like Nakht. He talked excitedly about everything he saw but not once did he mention his fall into the Nile.

By and by it was the season of Shemu, low water. It was the season of harvest, a time of rejoicing. The *fellahin*, farmers and land workers celebrated the harvest with a festival of music, singing, dancing, juggling, street entertainment, food hawkers and water sellers, which lasted the whole day and well into the night. Nakht had mentioned this coming festivity to Maya because, he said, she and Tut might enjoy it.

They could dress up as *fellahin* or servants.

It would be a pleasant change, he suggested, from Tut's and her usual routine. Maya, in seeking permission from Tiya, explained that Nakht would accompany them and in any event Tut was unlikely to be recognised. It would, Maya suggested, be a perfect opportunity for Tut to mix with his people; the ones he was not likely to come in contact with when he becomes king. Tiya, although concerned for her grandson's safety, gave in to the suppressed excitement in Maya's voice and granted permission on condition that Manetho, her head gardener, also accompany them.

In all the time Maya had been in Tiya's household she had never had cause to converse with Manetho. She had become aware of him when the old king passed away but not to speak to. She was therefore a little hesitant when she approached him. Having explained the situation and obtained his consent she ventured to ask him what his name meant.

"I am named after a well-known third-century Egyptian priest. I have no idea what the name itself means. I joined the priesthood at my mother's insistence when I was fourteen. That was where I learnt about gardening and the care of plants."

"Why did you leave?" asked Maya. Manetho

looked at Maya to ascertain her reason for the question. Seeing only youthful interest in her demeanour, he replied, "I could not stand all the rules and rituals. I do not believe in gods past or present, so when I heard the old king was looking for a gardener for his place in Thebes I applied and got the job."

She informed him of the time they planned to leave and the form of dress they would be assuming.

Maya borrowed a pair of large, round, earrings, a colourful scarf and a bright blue coarse cotton material which she wound round herself, leaving her shoulders bare. For Tut she acquired a tunic of stained cloth and a small kerchief for his head.

Maya advised Nakht to practice stooping a little, explaining he may give the game away since he looked every inch what he was, a soldier.

With everything in place, the borrowed clothing washed and ready, the day of the festival finally arrived. It was agreed they would leave mid-afternoon to travel to the village hosting the festivities. Tut knew nothing about the outing until he woke up from his rest and Maya was dressing him. He was beside himself with excitement especially when told Nakht would be with them. She explained he would have to pretend to be the son of a servant girl.

Whilst he turned his nose up at the clothes he had to put on he finally accepted, with much coaxing from Maya, that it was all part of the adventure and the only way he would be allowed to attend. She put some kohl round his eyes to ward off the evil eye and smudged some as dirt on his face and tied a kerchief round his head.

They met Swnwt on the stairs. She informed Maya Nakht had arrived and he and Manetho were waiting at the gate. Maya and Tut rushed down the rest of the stairs and into Tiya's quarters like a whirlwind.

"So, will we do?" said the two of them in unison. Tiya laughed at the sight.

"Serving girl and son. I would not have recognised either of you. I like the earrings, Maya. Take care and come back safely or I will have to answer to the King."

The two ran to the gate to see Nakht sitting on the seat of a wooden cart drawn by a plump donkey. Maya stared at it. All the donkeys she had seen around the City were emaciated, with protruding ribs.

"Where did you find this fat fellow?" she asked as she climbed into the cart.

"He belongs to the army," Nakht replied. Maya was about to introduce Manetho when Nakht interrupted her saying, "we have met and talked before on my visits to the villa."

Manetho, having assisted Maya and the Prince into the cart, climbed up beside Nakht. Maya explained that the servants had left straight after lunch so it was only the four of them. Tut was asking Maya questions about the festival. Since she had never been to one he gave up and asked Nakht instead. Tut was standing in the cart with his hands on Nakht's shoulders.

"There will be crowds of people milling around so you must stay close and not wander off. If you do Maya will never be allowed to bring you out again. Do you understand?" asked Nakht.

"Yes, Nakht" was the reply.

The journey across the city was uneventful and, apart from small groups making their way to the festival, quiet. As they got closer to the *fellahin* village they could hear the throbbing of drums, the tinkling of tambourines and the sound of lusty voices singing.

"What are they singing Nakht?" asked Maya.

"A harvest folk song."

Nakht stopped a little way from the village, took the donkey and cart to a clearing hidden by tall trees and bushes, where a young boy of about twelve years of age was waiting. Nakht tied the rope attached to the donkey and cart to a nearby tree and left the boy to keep watch while they were gone on promise of payment when they returned.

As the group drew closer to the crowd the atmosphere with the music, colourful clothing and noise of people enjoying themselves was intoxicating. Manetho suggested he put Tut on his shoulders so the Prince could see what was going on. Tut was the first to agree to this plan. He had never sat on anyone's shoulders before. Manetho held on to the child's legs until he was certain Tut was able to stay upright with his hands on Manetho's head.

Food hawkers were among the crowd selling spicy cooked chick peas, deep fried green peas, dried and salted watermelon seeds as well as dates, figs, and sweet meats. The threesome, with Tut riding high, wandered through the throng enjoying the carefree atmosphere. Once or twice Nakht caught hold of Maya's hand when they were going through a particularly thick throng of people ensuring also that Manetho and Tut were in front of him. She liked the touch of his hand; it was warm and reassuring.

After some time Maya gave in to Tut's persistent request to try the street food by getting some deep fried peas for all of them. It was served in small clay pots which were thrown away after use. They all agreed it was delicious. When Tut asked for a drink from the water-seller however Maya refused, taking out the leather bottle she had in her cloth bag and giving him a drink from that.

They came across a vendor selling wooden toys and Nakht bought Tut a small chariot complete with, unpainted, wooden horses. Tut, noted Maya, seemed more excited by the present Nakht bought him than anything he had ever received from his father. Just then Maya felt eyes on her. Looking up she noticed a woman staring at her and the Prince. She whispered to Nakht who calmly looked in the woman's direction.

"That is the Queen's head housekeeper. I think she recognises me and, from the look on her face, she suspects who you and Tut are. We better make our way back."

Nakht mentioned this to Manetho and the two started zig-zagging their way through the crowd. Within a matter of minutes Nakht felt the hairs on the back of his neck rise.

As he turned he saw two well-built men, just behind him, hauling away another man into the crowd. Unsure of what was going on Nakht offered to carry Tut and the party quickened its pace back to where the cart was tethered.

"Nakht, did you notice the disturbance just behind

us whilst we were leaving the festivities?" asked Maya.

"Yes. All three men were built like soldiers. Strange."

"I did not see anything," said Manetho.

"You were in front of me looking ahead," responded Nakht.

The boy was still there, laid out on the ground near the donkey's head, feeding it blades of grass he had pulled up from the earth. He got up when he saw Nakht, who patted the boy on his shoulder and paid him with a coin.

By the time they got back to the villa Tut had fallen asleep. Manetho kindly took Tut to his room where Swnwt was waiting to prepare him for bed. Before going up Maya thanked Nakht for making the outing possible and offered to recompense him for the money spent on the toy.

"You should not have to use your own resources," said Maya.

Nakht refused her offer.

"I have come to love that child and it is a privilege to spend time with him. It is a small price to pay for the pleasure I derive from both his and your company. Also it's a going away present."

"What do you mean?" asked Maya, rather too

anxiously.

"I move out with the army tomorrow. The Nubians are rebelling and not paying their tribute so the King has ordered Horemheb to quell the troubles and bring back the outstanding taxes."

"We shall miss you. How long will you be gone?"

"I am not sure. It could be a year or more. Will you tell Tut goodbye for me?"

"Yes, of course. I will explain the reason for your absence. Will you write to us and let us know how you are getting on?"

"I am unable to get any letters to you. Only despatches to the King are allowed when we are on campaign."

"Goodbye, little brother," said Maya feeling more pain than she could explain to herself. "May the gods keep you safe."

With that she turned and ran into the house. Tears were rolling down her cheeks which she brushed away hurriedly as she went up the stairs to check on Tut.

Later, when she was calm, having washed and changed into a loose fine cotton gown, she went to Tiya's sitting room. The beautiful elderly woman was curled up in her favourite chair, reading. It was clear from her face that she welcomed the interruption.

The two retired officers on special assignment to protect the young Prince kept a firm hold on their captive, half dragging, half carrying him to their hiding place where two others were waiting with horses. The captive was bound and thrown onto a horse. The two who had captured him rode off with their prisoner in tow while the other two skirted round the village to where they knew Nakht had left the cart. They shadowed the Prince's party until it safely entered the gates of the villa.

Having reached the Royal Palace, the prisoner was taken to the dungeon where his arms and legs were shackled to the wall. One soldier kept watch on the prisoner while the other reported to the King who had not long returned to his rooms from the Government Palace. He was just about to carry out his evening ablutions.

As the soldier was shown in the King dismissed his body servant. "What news?" he asked wearily.

The old soldier made his report. "As Nakhtmia and his party were making their way back to their conveyance a man came up behind them, dagger drawn. As he raised his arm it became clear he was aiming for the young Prince who was on the shoulders of the man in front of Nakhtmia. We moved forward and dragged the attacker away without the party realising there was any danger. He is in the dungeon. He refuses to say anything. He looks like a mercenary, a seasoned fighter. Do you wish to question him, Highness?"

"Try persuasion. It is important we find out who he is working for. If that does not work put him in a safe place. I will interrogate him tomorrow. My son is safe?"

"Yes, Highness."

"My mother seems determined to raise him to be fearless," remarked the King. He dismissed the soldier and hit the gong summoning his body servant.

In the dungeon, the two set to work on the would-be assassin. They used the whip, hot tongs on his feet and various other torture methods. All he would say was, "It matters not whether I live or die; my family are well provided for as long as I remain silent."

Not wanting to deprive the King the opportunity to question the prisoner, they decided to cease the interrogation when he lost consciousness for the third time. They dragged him to a hole in the bowels of the Palace and chained him to the wall. Believing he would be safe there until morning the two left.

The following morning as the captors went to check on the prisoner, prior to reporting to the King, they found him sleeping. On closer inspection they realised he was not breathing. Looking around the ground they found an empty vial.

"This is the work of someone who knows his way around these dungeons. Look at his skin, it's discoloured, and there is froth at the corners of the mouth suggesting strong poison," observed the older of the two. "The King will not be pleased. We had better inform him immediately."

In the meantime Poly reported to the Queen her sighting of the Prince at the festivities.

"A missed opportunity, Poly," she said. "We should have thought about that possibility. Well, *you* should have."

"My Queen, I had no way of knowing they would be in such a public place. Nothing was said in Swnwt's last report."

Chapter 10

Before Maya could tell of their afternoon adventure Tiya said,

"Maya, I think it is time Tut learned about the priesthood of Amun; their code of ethics and what their duties are. He can only do so at Karnak. Even though it's officially closed I can arrange for him to meet the High Priest who will instruct him. It may also be useful for him to learn, at this time, about the public calendar and how it is made up."

"I have been meaning to ask you to arrange for a young astrologer to attend and teach Tut the basics about the stars and their importance to Egyptian life" said Maya.

"That is a good thought. I will organise it with the High Priest. He will know which priest to send and which night will be most auspicious for such learning. Now, what were you going to tell me?"

Maya related the events of the afternoon but not wishing to disturb Tiya's peace of mind, made no mention of their group being seen by the Queen's housekeeper. She also reported Nakht's imminent departure.

"All the more reason for us to keep Tut occupied," said his Nana.

The next day Tiya sent a trusted servant to Karnak with her request, making clear the need for caution and secrecy so as not to anger her son. Tiya also had another thought which she now acted upon. She sent for Manetho who was busy in the garden planting more lilies in the pond and generally cleaning it out. He went to his quarters, washed his hands and face and changed out of his gardening clothes before entering the villa.

Tiya greeted him with a smile and pointed to the armchair opposite her own.

"Did you enjoy the outing yesterday?"

"Very much. I have never been married and have no children. I was surprised how much pleasure I derived from carrying the young Prince on my shoulder and pointing out the different activities going on."

"What would you think about being a companion to the Prince when he goes out for lessons? You will have to be sworn to secrecy and will also have to guard the Prince with your life."

Manetho remained silent with a thoughtful look on his face. He felt sure the mistress had more to say.

"I understand from Maya," continued Tiya, "that you were a member of the priesthood for many years. Can I then trust you to take the Prince to the temple at Karnak one day a week, to wait there and bring him back? I will make all travel arrangements and let you know week by week which day he will be going. It will, for obvious reasons, not be the same day each week. If you agree to do this you have my permission to appoint a deputy to carry out some of your gardening duties."

Manetho raised from his seat and walked to the window overlooking the front garden, arms folded in front of his broad chest. After a couple of minutes he turned calm, untroubled eyes on Mistress Tiya.

"I do not believe in gods. Could you still trust me to protect the life of the future Pharaoh?"

"Yes. I have faith in your ability to protect my grandson. So long as you keep your lack of belief to yourself I cannot think of a more capable companion. Will you accept this task?"

"Yes."

"Excellent. It will take time to organise. We will talk further."

Manetho returned to his quarters, changed back into his work clothes and walked slowly back to the garden pond. He marvelled to himself how quickly life could change after staying the same for years on end. The first time this happened was when he decided to leave the priesthood. Now he was being elevated from gardener to bodyguard to the future King.

While Tiya was making arrangements, Maya started to prepare Tut without actually telling him of his Nana's plans. The boy reacted badly to being told Nakht would be away for some time. He sulked, would not do as he was asked and even went off his food.

Maya assured him that when he was older he would have to leave her in order to train to be a leader and a soldier and would have to go on campaigns also. It would, she assured him, be her turn to be sad until he returned safely. She explained he had much to learn before he became King. She kept Tut busy by involving him in preparing a timetable for his lessons.

The first subject was the gods of Egypt. Maya referred to the plan Tiya had drawn for her. They agreed to have the lesson in the garden, under the shade near the pond.

"First of all, Tut, I will tell you a little about the religion your father follows and then I will teach you about Amun, the religion that has been followed in Egypt for hundreds of years, which your father banned."

"Gidu called Father a heretic," interjected Tut.

Maya thought it prudent not to respond to Tut's remark.

"Your father, in order to stop the priests interfering in his rule, decided to ban all the gods of the land and to introduce a new god, the Aten. This god is shown as a large round disc with rays of light emanating from it and is called a solar disc, meaning sun.

"The Pharaoh explained," she said, "that the rays of the sun stopped in his hands which meant he held all life in the form of the ankh, the key of life. It follows, from this change, that only the Pharaoh has access to the God Aten.

"Thus priests are no longer required. Your father closed all public temples, including the temple at Karnak and took all its lands, ships and treasurers into his own royal treasury."

"Gidu told me about that," said Tut. "He wants me to change everything back when I am Pharaoh."

Maya nodded and continued. "That is why your father built this new capital city, to get away completely from the Amun priesthood. Let us have lunch now. Later I will explain about Amun."

After the two had taken lunch with Tiya and rested, the lesson continued indoors. Maya recapped what Tut had learned in the morning.

As Maya repeated what Tiya had told her about

the god Amun she could see Tut's eyes glazing over. He was losing interest.

"Don't worry, you will learn this in more detail later. You just need to hear it at least once now so it is not so strange when you hear it again. Come on, let's have a game of catch in the garden. It's cooler now."

That night Tut dreamed of floating across the sky in a boat. To his surprise it was not Maya in the boat with him but a slender, beautiful young woman with thick dark wavy hair and an angelic smile. She had her arms around his shoulders and her head close to his. He felt safe and happy.

"Are you a god?" he asked.

"No," she smiled. "I am your mother. We have met before in your dreams."

"Why did you have to leave me, Mama?" Before she could answer the dream faded and Tut woke up, distressed. Maya came into his room and comforted him.

"How long did you know my mother Maya?"

"We grew up together. We were best friends."

"Why did she leave me?" asked Tut, eyes brimming with tears.

"She did not want to leave you. She was taken by the gods. She had no choice. Remember what I said to you before? Like your Gidu, while your mother is in your heart and in your thoughts it means you remember her and as long as you remember, she has not left you. Just think, she will never grow old or suffer pain and the two of you will be together again one day if you honour the gods and live a good life."

She laid Tut back in bed and gave him a warm hug.

"Your mother left me to take care of you and I will until I die," said Maya, fighting back tears.

Chapter 11

"Your father presented you with scarab beetle jewellery on your last birthday," said Maya, pulling out a scarab ring and brooch from a pouch full of children's jewellery. "It is believed that the scarab beetle holds magical powers and can bring royalty, such as you Tut, back to life. Many pieces of scarab jewellery are buried with dead Pharaohs."

Tut took the ring and tried it on. It was too big. "Pin the brooch on my tunic Maya. I really like it."

"Try the gold chain on also," suggested Maya "Look, it has the ankh attached for protection. It is not a good idea to play outside with such jewellery on but you can wear them indoors."

"Continuing the theme of the gods," said Maya, "priests of Amun say the gods favour people with large families. Couples without children are thought of as selfish especially if they do not adopt orphan children to fill the gap in their lives.

Did I tell you I was brought up in King Tushratta's orphanage until your mother took a liking to me and chose me to be her companion?"

"No," replied Tut. "Did you not know your mother either?" Tut's face looked sad.

"No," said Maya. "That is why I understand so well how you feel not having your mother. The High

Priest of Amun will be able to give you a fuller explanation of the gods."

"How can he when the temples are closed?" asked Tut.

"Your Nana is arranging it," replied Maya.

The day arrived for Tut to be taken by Manetho to Karnak. Manetho wore his oldest gardening clothes and Tut was dressed in an old tunic, much to the child's disgust. A tunic of fine linen and his royal headdress were stowed away in a bag for him to wear when he reached his destination. Tut rode a donkey and Manetho a sturdy horse. A soft cloth had been placed over the donkey's back so that the Prince's inner thighs would not rub against the donkey's rough hairs.

They travelled along the back roads, starting out after an early breakfast and reached Karnak before the sun was at its zenith. Manetho, armed with a club and a heavy stick, remained vigilant throughout the journey. Although he saw no-one he was convinced they were being watched. He managed to control his fear for the Prince's safety and chatted with his charge about the vegetables he had recently planted in the rear garden at the villa.

From outside, the imposing temple building

appeared deserted. Manetho led his horse and Tut's donkey to a side entrance where a lesser priest was waiting to take the animals. Another priest escorted them to the High Priest's office building. As they followed, Manetho could see priests working in the fields, the gardens and in the workshops to the side of the inner courtyard. There was a quiet buzz of industry. The flower gardens were well tended and to the left Manetho could see a set of bee hives. He experienced a feeling of stepping back in time.

They reached a large square building and the priest ushered them into a room where the two were able to wash the dust off their hands and face and have the bread, cheese and drink Maya had packed for them. Tut changed into his tunic and Pharaohnic head dress. They were then taken to the High Priest.

They walked along a clean corridor, following the same priest who had brought them in, until they came to a large, highly polished wooden door. The priest knocked before opening the heavy door. Inside, the room was cool and sparsely furnished. There was a large desk near the south wall, a comfortable looking chair behind it and stools scattered around. Behind the desk was a smaller door.

A very tall, broad man of middle years came towards

them, arms outstretched. He had a large square face with big, sticking out ears, a big nose, large eyes and a kind, full, mouth. He was dressed in a full length, white, linen tunic and white sandals on his large feet. His head, face and arms were clean shaven.

"I am Athosis, High Priest of Amun," he said in a warm bass voice as he took Tut's hands in his.

"When you are Pharaoh, Prince, you will be the High Priest and I your Deputy."

Tut studied Athosis's face but said nothing. The High Priest let go of Tut's hands gently.

"Am I correct in thinking, Manetho, your journey here was uneventful?" asked Athosis.

"Yes. However, I had a distinct impression we were being watched." Tut looked at Manetho, surprised.

"You were clearly being watched over by the gods," responded Athosis.

"Do you have any objection to me looking around, perhaps helping in the garden while His Highness is with you?" asked Manetho. Athosis looked at Tut, who in turn looked at Manetho.

"I will be safe here" said Tut.When they were alone, Athosis pulled up a couple of stools and invited Tut to sit.

"Why do you think we have temples?"

Tut shrugged his shoulders.

"It is to ensure the gods' presence on earth. Why would we want to ensure the gods' presence?" asked Athosis.

Tut shrugged again.

"The gods' presence maintains the harmonious order of the world as the gods created it. The Egyptian people strive to live good lives in the hope of earning merit for the life to come," explained Athosis.

"As the King you will be the only one entitled to immediate contact with the gods, since you will be a living god. However, your priests can carry out all the duties required of you by the gods.

"There is a high priest for each god. *Sem*, senior priests, carry out the god's daily ablution rituals and religious rites. These are carried out every day in temples throughout the realm. In time I will show you the drawings on the temple walls where the Pharaoh is drawn as large as the gods themselves. This is because the King is of the same standing as the gods.

"Training for the priesthood starts at age fourteen. Before a young man can enter the priesthood he has to be circumcised for the sake of cleanliness."

Tut did not understand the word 'circumcised' but decided to ask Maya rather than interrupt the High Priest. The boy was fascinated by Athosis's large nose and sticky-out ears and it took all his self-control not to continue staring at them.

"The entire body," continued the High Priest, "has to be shaven, including eyebrows and eye lashes to avoid danger of lice or any other uncleanliness. Do you know what food priests eat?"

"No." Not sure where to look, Tut focused on Athosis's chin.

"It differs depending on the god but here at the temple of Amun we are not allowed to eat the meat of cows. Neither can we eat mutton, pork, pigeon, pelican, Nile perch or sea fish because they may be gods incarnate. We are also not allowed to eat beans, garlic, green stuff or salt. We usually have geese or fowl, bread, cheese, onions, pulses and some vegetables, and we are allowed grape wine in small quantities.

"Young priests wear pure white kilts woven from clean, fine linen and white sandals. They are allowed to marry but must follow the temple's purifying rules before entering the inner sanctum of the gods.

"The Temple's code is clear:
Never enter the temple in a state of impurity or sin;
Lay no false charges;
Have no interest in profit;
Accept no bribes;

Do not spurn the lowly in favour of the mighty;
Use no false measure of weight;
Tell no gossip about the rites you perform since they are
sacred secrets special to the temple.

Have you any questions so far, Prince?"

"Yes. Are the *fellahin* allowed in the temple?" asked Tut remembering the harvest festival.

"No, Highness, only the King, his priests and certain noblemen are allowed into the temple. Others can only enter the forecourt to bring offerings, ask for prayers to be said for them and their family or to pursue a legal claim."

"So the closing of the temples have not affected the poor people?"

"I would say not," replied Athosis. "The next time we meet I will show you around the temple complex. After that I will arrange for you to experience what is involved in the usual temple services. Would you agree that is enough for now?"

"Yes," answered Tut. "But how are you able to continue with services when my father has taken your lands and treasures?"

"A good question. This land was gifted by your grandfather who started the building of Karnak temple. The gift was expressed in such a way that it remains temple land for all time. As to our treasures, we grow most of what we eat, some goods we obtain by bartering. We still have many wealthy benefactors who continue to seek our services in saying prayers and making sacrifices for the protection of their families both alive and dead. Our astrologers also give readings and receive gifts for their service."

Athosis got up from the stool with a little difficulty and walked over to his desk. He picked up and rang a small bell which was sitting, unnoticed by Tut, on the right hand side of the High Priest's otherwise clear desk. The priest that had brought them appeared. Tut thanked Athosis and followed the priest out.

Maya had not been idle while Tut was away. Having sworn the gate keeper to secrecy, she dressed as a young man, pinning her shoulder length dark tresses close to her head, putting on a cap popular with young men of learning and going into the city.

As she made her way through the narrow, unfamiliar streets, trying not to make eye contact with anyone, she noted many richly dressed men on beautiful Arabian horses, alongside others, not so well-dressed, on unkempt horses. Traders with loaded carts pulled by small donkeys, stopped at intervals to call out for customers. As she got closer to the Government Palace she saw scribes with pallets slung across their shoulders hurrying this way and that. *Fellahin* were busy sprinkling water to settle the sandy dust. Others were sweeping the steps of the Government Palace.

Not far from the Government Palace Maya found the House of Life where medicine and astronomy are studied and the public calendar set. As she entered she noted, to her right, a display of medical instruments.

Knives, forceps and both wooden and metal probes used in surgery were on show, along with instruments used in dentistry for removing and implanting teeth.

Maya, who was studying the instruments, jumped when a young man came up to her and said, "Are you attending medical school also?"

"No, no," she said in a gruff voice. "I am a visitor here and I have heard so much about Egyptian medicine that I wanted to have a look for myself."

"My name is Gwa. My father is a doctor and as the elder son I am expected to follow the same profession. I would prefer to be a soldier but that choice is not open to me."

"Why don't you become a doctor and then join the army" suggested Maya.

Gwa peered at Maya. "You sound like my sister."

Maya laughed as gruffly as she could manage. "Ah," she said, "women do sometimes talk sense."

"May I show you around?"

"That would be a kindness," replied Maya.

"These scrolls over here contain all the rules of medicine written so far. If a doctor follows these rules in treating his patient he is not held responsible if he cannot save the patient.

"If, however, he tries something new, going against what is written, and his patient dies, he would have to submit to trial for murder, with death as a penalty if found guilty."

"All the more reason to be an army doctor." remarked Maya. "More freedom to try new ideas on the battle field."

"True," conceded Gwa.

"Over here we have a growing, written collection of medicines used for treating internal diseases. The scrolls are arranged according to the organ concerned. Do you know, a severe injury to the skull can cause discharge of blood from ones ears and nose?"

Maya pulled a face and nodded, intimating "No."

Gwa continued. "Egyptians believe the heart to be the site of the soul and the reasoning faculty which dictate ones quality of character and emotions. I want to concentrate on the upper part of the body, the organ near the heart and the main bones down the back. I especially want to find a cure for the widespread ailment which causes water to build up in and around the upper part of the body, especially in men. I have also noted problems in the main back bone, which in some cases leads to a hump developing."

"Then you should work as a quarry or tomb workers' doctor," suggested Maya.

Gwa looked at Maya with a slight frown. "Are you sure you know nothing about medicine?" he asked

"No, I do not but I have plenty of common sense."

"My sister says men are short on common sense. She would enjoy meeting you."

"I do not wish to offend but I am particularly interested in seeing the public calendar," said Maya changing the subject. Is there one on display?"

"Yes. On the floor above. Come, I will take you."

As they were making their way up the stairs Maya noticed several clean-shaven young men, wearing priests garb, white kilts and white sandals.

"Do you get many priests visiting?" she asked.

"The priests who come to The House of Life are training to be doctors, dentists, astronomers or astrologers.

"Ah, here is a painting of Sakhmet, the goddess or

patroness of diseases," said Gwa as they reached the next floor.

"Is this not the astronomer's floor?" she asked.

"Yes, it is and over on this wall," Gwa said, pointing to his left, "is the current Public Calendar. The Calendar was established for administrative purposes," he explained. "The year is divided into twelve months. Each month has thirty days. Five extra days are then added to the year. These are called Epagomenal days and correspond to the birthdays of the gods Osiris, Set, Horus and of the goddesses Isis and Nephthys.

"The problem with the lunar calendar," continued Gwa, "is that it lags behind the solar year by one day every four years. The astronomers have not yet worked out how to get round that difficulty."

Maya listened carefully in order to remember all Gwa was telling her about the public calendar since she would have to explain it to Tut.

Glancing out of the window Maya realised it was time she left if she was to get back to the villa before nightfall.

"I must leave now," she said to Gwa. "Thank you for your company and for being so helpful."

Before Gwa could reply Maya was on her way down the stairs.

He called after her, "But I don't know your name."

She did not look back but quickened her pace and made for the exit. She stopped outside to get her bearings.

"Phew! What an interesting day," thought Maya as she hurried back towards the villa.

The streets seemed less busy now. She noticed one of the beggars relieving his bowels at the side of the roadway. She quickly looked ahead of her and walked a bit faster, pretending not to notice.

Maya entered the villa via the servants' entrance and managed to get to her room unnoticed. She flopped on her bed and heaved a sigh of relief. That was her first lone adventure and she had enjoyed it apart from the plight of the poor which distressed her.

"What have you been doing with your free time?" asked Tiya as she watched Maya skipping down the stairs like a young girl.

"I was wondering the same about you," said Maya.

"When is Tut due back?"

"Should be any time now. Shall we sit in the garden and await his return? I was just on my way out there."

The two ladies wandered out into the garden and sat where they could watch the fishes in the pond chase each other.

"Are you warm enough, Tiya? I will get you a shawl."

"Thank you, Maya. There is one on the arm of the chair in my resting room." Maya jumped up and ran into the house. No sooner was she out with the shawl when the Prince arrived.

The boy was tired and hungry. After he had greeted his Nana Maya took him in for a bath and something to eat.

Manetho called one of the male servants to see to the animals and, with Tiya's permission, sat down. He made his report and handed her a letter sent by the High Priest.

Tiya opened the scroll and read it with difficulty in the fading light. "It seems Athosis is pleased with his pupil. He is complimentary about you also, Manetho."

"I only gave one of his gardeners some advice on how to look after the fruit trees that were recently planted."

"Well, it's a good start. My grandson looked very tired. How was he on the trip?"

"He showed an interest in everything around him and did not complain once on the journey even though his bottom and legs were sore on the way back."

For reasons he could not articulate Manetho decided not to share his suspicion of being followed but resolved instead to seek permission to take a sturdy under-gardener along on future outings.

"Thank you, Manetho. I will let you know when the next visit has been arranged. Good night."

Tut was too tired to talk much. He allowed himself to be washed and managed a glass of warm milk with a slice of bread and honey before falling asleep. Despite sitting on the soft cloth, his inner thighs were chapped and his bottom sore from the time spent on the donkey's back.

That night Tut dreamt of flying donkeys with big sticking-out ears.

Maya dreamt about Gwa saying, "You sound like my sister". In her sleep she decided she needed to practice sounding more masculine before she ventured out in disguise again.

The next morning Maya rubbed Tut's inner thighs and bottom with an ointment sent by Manetho. Tut remembered he had a question.

"Maya, what does 'circumcision' mean?"

Maya stopped in her tracks and blinked, wondering whether she had heard right. "Why do you ask?"

"The High Priest mentioned it."

"It's a ceremony all young men go through when they reach the age of fourteen. Do you remember me telling you to pull back the foreskin on your implement," she said, pointing to his penis, "and washing it thoroughly?"

Tut looked down at his penis, his cotton pants half way up his legs, and then at Maya questioningly.

"Well", she continued, getting a little red in the face, "in order to be clean, when a boy reaches the age of fourteen, the priest cuts that foreskin and frees the head of his implement."

"Oh." Tut screwed up his face. "That sounds painful."

"It is, but a young man has to learn to handle pain just as he must learn to handle happiness, sadness, hunger or thirst. You will be king and a warrior one day so it is important for you to be able to control your feelings, both good and bad."

"I will be able to control myself but I am not having that done to me," said Tut. "Maya, the High Priest recited the Temple Code to me. The one I remember best says not to spurn the lowly in favour of the mighty."

Maya, feeling a little uncomfortable at ignoring the beggars the previous day, looked at Tut questioningly.

"There are servants' children here," he said. "The same ones that were at Nana's palace yet I have never spoken with them let alone play with them. Why?"

"You have never spoken to or played with any high born children either Tut" she replied.

"True but why have I not done so?"

"Your father and Nana want to keep you safe from illness, that is why you do not mix with other children. Also the servants are afraid to let their children play with you while you are so young. You may get hurt or injured. They fear for their position in your Nana's household. They know your Nana would not treat them unfairly but have no wish to put that belief to the test. Besides you are royalty and cannot afford the luxury of random friendships.

"Right my Prince, let us have some breakfast and you can tell your Nana and I all you learned yesterday."

Chapter 12

Swnwt had, over the past weeks, noticed the Prince leaving the villa accompanied by Manetho and one of the under gardeners and not returning until evening looking very tired. She had included this fact in her monthly report for fear the Queen may learn of it from her other possible sources which could place Swnwt in danger of the Queen's wrath. She had received instructions to ascertain where the Prince was going on his days out.

Swnwt had searched Tut's quarters but that had yielded no clues. She had tried to strike up a friendship with Manetho but he was very reserved and made it clear he was not interested. Swnwt had decided long ago she would only marry a man who could improve her position in palace society. She had had reasonable prospects of meeting such a man when she worked at the palace with young diplomats and courtiers coming and going. She had, however, given up on that dream when she joined Tut's household.

She acknowledged to herself that Manetho was the best looking male in Lady Tiya's household with prospects to better himself if he chose to but he stirred no feelings in her. She was not complaining, it could prove profitable to be close to the future Pharaoh. She was well aware of the dangers of her current position and was concerned not to arouse suspicion in either the Queen's or Maya's mind.

She needed to get the child on his own. She thought of a plan and approached Maya after breakfast the day following his outing. She hinted that Tut looked weary and perhaps a morning painting would do him good. She related to Maya a promise she had made to Tut some time ago to explain the meaning of the different colours.

Maya had, of late, found herself warming to Swnwt. In the time she had been with them Maya had found no reason for mistrusting her. She sensed Swnwt was genuinely fond of Tut which softened her heart towards the girl.

"That sounds like a good idea. I know he enjoys painting. I will get some broken jugs and scraps of papyrus. You get the paints and bring Tut to the garden."

Before long Tut and Swnwt were sitting at a table in the garden setting out water and paints.

Manetho was moving around on the far side tending the fruit trees like a father fussing around his children. His face was a picture of concentration. His aura, that of a man content with his lot in life.

"Young Master, I have brought nine different

colours already mixed. Shall we start with red?"

"Red is one of my favourite colours," said Tut.

"Red is a mixture of ochre and haematite - no, I am not sure what that is either, young Master. Red represents the blood of life. It is also the colour used for evil or violence."

"Does that mean I am evil and violent for liking red?"

"No, no," replied Swnwt. It means you love being alive. Blue," she continued, "is made by mixing copper, silicate or cobalt salt and is used for colouring the sky, the hair of gods and lapis lazuli. Turquoise is for youth and freshness. Yellow is used to represent gold, the body of gods and eternity. Pale yellow, which is a mixture of ochre and arsenic sulphate, is used for colouring the female complexion.

"Brownish red is used for the male complexion. White is made from plaster or chalk and is used to represent light, dawn, luxury and joy. Green is malachite mixed with lime and is used to represent water, grass and the leaves on the trees. Black is made by mixing charcoal and soot and represents the black earth, its fertility, riches and the life to come.

"All these colours are water-based with gum Arabic and the white of eggs added as a bond. We can now also get paints bonded with bees wax. Shall we do some painting now?"

While the child was applying red paint to the square piece of broken earthenware, Swnwt remarked casually, in a conversational tone,

"The household really miss you when you go off for the whole day. Where do you go?"

Tut looked at the beautiful young woman sitting beside him, at her shining head of thick dark hair; her soft, smooth olive-coloured skin and her large, rich brown eyes glowing with warmth.

"Oh," replied Tut, "that is no secret. Manetho is teaching me to ride. We go to the stables of a friend of his in the desert. It's great fun but very tiring."

Tut was pleased to see that Swnwt believed him. Manetho had done a good job of coaching him on what to say if anyone asked about his time away from the villa. Swnwt did not ask any further questions and the two enjoyed the painting session.

When the information was passed to the Queen she saw the opportunity she had been waiting for ever since Poly had reported seeing the Prince at the harvest festival. Swnwt had been closely questioned on the Queen's instructions. From her interrogation, Poly was convinced Swnwt knew nothing of that outing beforehand.

At last, a chance to despatch the boy to the underworld, thought the Queen. No one could suspect her of foul play if Tut, while in disguise, is attacked and both he and his companions are killed.

Once again the Queen summoned her trusted housekeeper.

"Poly, I need you to find me a couple of *fellahin* that can be trusted to keep watch on Mistress Tiya's villa, to follow the man called Manetho and the young boy with him when they go out together, and kill them. It must look like a robbery and they must get the job done without any mistakes. They have to be men without ties to the city who would be willing to leave once the deed is done. I will see they are well rewarded. However, make it clear, if they breathe a word of the act to anyone, I will ensure they do not live to enjoy their pay."

As the gods would have it, Kara, one of the Queen's maids, was in the cupboard next to where the Queen and her housekeeper were talking. Kara was putting away clean linen and towels. When she heard voices she kept very still and listened intently to the conversation.

After the talking ceased she waited some time before venturing out of the linen cupboard. The coast was clear. She went straight to her room in the servants' quarters to think.

The only young boy at Mistress Tiya's villa, apart from the servants' children," she reasoned, "is the Prince."

She must inform the King. She decided to leave the agreed mark, a small red sash, fashioned in the form of an ankh, hung on the inside of the door handle to the anteroom which the King had to pass through to get to his private apartment.

Kara managed to leave the mark for the King without being seen since his Elite Guards were in and near the state room. She then resolved to stay in her room for the rest of the day if need be. She could not risk giving anything away by accident. She decided if she was challenged by the housekeeper she would say she had a bad belly ache and felt faint.

It was an hour before one of the other maids came to her room.

"We have been looking for you everywhere. The laundry mistress expected you back. She is very angry."

Kara, arms wrapped round her belly, explained the reason for her absence. The maid went off to report back. It was late in the afternoon, Kara was pacing up and down her small room trying not to think about how hungry she was when there came a sharp knock on her door. She put one arm across her tummy and with the other she opened to door carefully. There stood the King's personal secretary. He beckoned to her to follow him.

When she was alone with the King he said, "What is it Kara? This is the first time you have used the emergency arrangement we have. What have you discovered?"

Kara related the conversation between the Queen and her housekeeper almost word for word.

"You did the right thing, Kara. I will make sure you are well rewarded."

"My concern, Highness, is for the safety of the young Prince."

"Well said. Leave it with me. I have safety provisions in place. However, your information is most helpful. Go about your duties but keep your eyes and ears open and your mouth closed."

She bowed and left.

Chapter 13

Left alone, the King heaved a heartfelt sigh. He loved and admired his wife. She was beautiful, intelligent and articulate yet her jealousy blinded her. She could not see clearly where Tut was concerned. Enough of this introspection, he said to himself.

The King summoned Djer, the Captain of his Elite Guards, and related to him the plot against the Prince without revealing the source of the danger. They discussed what was needed in order to ensure the Prince's safety.

The day following the painting lesson with Swnwt, Tut sought Manetho out. Maya was with his Nana and they were both being secretive. Tut found Manetho applying horse manure to the roots of the trees. Tut wrinkled his nose at the smell.

"Good morning, young Master," hailed Manetho. "Is the smell getting to you? It is good feed for the trees, ensuring healthy, plentiful fruits." Noting Tut was turning pale in his effort not to breathe in the stink, Manetho asked, "Do you wish to talk to me about something in particular?"

"I am not sure if it is important but yesterday Swnwt asked me where I go when I leave the villa with you. I told her what you advised me to say which, in any case, will be true when I turn five.

"You were right to mention it. Bring your bow, arrows and boomerang when we next leave the villa. Just in case.

"What do you think might happen Manetho?"

"Nothing might happen but it is better to be prepared."

"I will increase practicing with my bow and arrows," said Tut, excited at the thought of a dangerous adventure, forgot the stench of the manure.

Just then Maya walked down the steps of the villa to see where Tut was. She waved at him to come to her.

"Come on young man," she called. "I have to teach you today about the public calendar and the number of days in the year." Tut ran over to her, looked at her adoringly and followed her into the villa.

Not long after, Tiya came out and sat on the seat surrounded by bright, colourful flowers. The scent of jasmine caressed her senses. She and Maya had been discussing Tut's fifth birthday which was fast approaching. Maya wanted to hire an entertainer. Tiya agreed to seek her son's agreement and to ask whether some young nobles of Tut's age could be invited. She was mindful of the potential danger of having palace dignitaries at the villa with easy access to Tut.

After further thought, Tiya decided she would not mention to her son having other children at Tut's birthday celebrations. Safer, she decided, to wait until Tut was older.

As Tiya was reviewing these thoughts, eyes closed and enjoying the warmth of the sun, she became aware of a shadow blocking the light. Looking up, she smiled.

"Good day, Manetho. What can I help you with?"

"May I sit down?" She pointed to the space opposite her and waited.

"The young Master told me Swnwt asked him where he and I go on the days we leave without Maya. He told her he goes horse riding with me and, he said, she seemed to believe him. Should we be concerned?"

"It may be nothing but we cannot assume so. You do have a friend who runs a stable just outside the City?"

"Yes."

"Can you contact him and arrange for you and Tut to visit in order to choose a horse on which Tut can start learning to ride? His fifth birthday is only thirty days away."

Manetho nodded assent.

"Maya has always been suspicious of Swnwt but until now has found no cause. She was only telling me this morning that Swnwt seems to have a true affection for Tut."

"She may have but there are forces at work here that can bend a servant girl to its will," said Manetho.

"True enough," agreed Tiya. "We must be vigilant. When can we expect fruit from those trees you have been tending so lovingly?"

"It will not be too long before you are enjoying fresh plums, pomegranates, dates and figs. All in their right season of course. The vegetable garden is already supplying most of the villa's greens and vegetables."

Tiya smiled at the note of pride in Manetho's voice; it was a rare show of feeling. "I see you are keeping the under gardeners busy weeding and feeding the plants also."

"Ah, you have got a whiff of the manure then."

"The jasmine is doing a good job of masking the smell on this side of the garden. I suspect what I am smelling is emanating from your boots and kilt."

Manetho laughed. "That is my cue to take my leave of you and get back to my work."

"I will let Maya know the situation," said Tiya as Manetho got up to leave.

Chapter 14

As promised Tiya arranged for an apprentice astronomer to attend the villa to teach Tut the basics about the stars. Thus it was that a young man attended the villa one afternoon to arrange when he could give Tut his first lesson.

Maya and Tut were in the garden when he arrived. Maya thought he looked between fourteen and sixteen years old; he was tall and thin, with a slender face to match his long arms and legs. He was clean-shaven from the head down and dressed in a short white kilt tied in the style of a priest with matching white sandals. The young man introduced himself as Seni and explained he was a priest apprentice to a Master Astronomer in the House of Learning.

Tiya, hearing voices, came and joined them. Maya introduced her to Seni. They sat under the shade by the fish pond and Tiya rang for pomegranate juice to be brought.

"Seni," said Tiya "what made you choose to study astronomy?"

"As I was growing up my mother teased me that I was becoming so tall no doubt I would be able to touch the stars one day. This led me to spending time on the roof of our home staring at the crowded sky and wondering whether the stars had names. I just had to find out what was going on up there."

The drink having arrived Maya poured the ruby liquid into long glasses. "Tell us Seni" said Maya "what sort of night is best for star gazing?"

"You need a clear night with no moon for the best view," he replied, taking a sip of the welcome drink. "We have just had a full moon so the new moon cycle starts again. The next few nights will be ideal. I will check with the lunar calendar and my teacher and send a message as to which evening I will come. It will be after sundown. Will that be in order Prince?"

Tut looked at Maya who nodded slightly. "Yes, that will be in order."

The next day Maya and Tut had a practice run. Tut had his nap later in the afternoon, a light meal at sunset and when it was dark the two of them made their way to the roof, leaving a lamp on the top stair.

They lay on cushions Maya had brought up earlier in the day and looked up at the star-studded sky. The part of the sky that caught both their attention was that which looked like a long milky strip, thick with twinkling stars, some making shapes and patterns.

"It would be so interesting to know the names of some of those celestial bodies," said Maya. Tut was overcome with the beauty of what he saw.

"How is it I have never noticed this amazing

display in our night sky before, Maya?"

"Because you are usually in bed asleep. As you get older you will, I am sure, come to learn its secrets. Seni will be giving you an introduction. There is nothing to stop us coming up here on a clear night now that you are getting older."

On the fifth evening after his visit, as his note stated, Seni attended the Prince after sundown. The three of them ascended the stairs to the roof.

"Now Prince, let your eyes become accustomed to the dark. Look up in that direction," said Seni, pointing North. "Can you see that really bright star to the left? That is the North Star, which is always visible and is called the Imperishable One. That is the star sailors and travellers look for to ensure they are travelling in the right direction."

Tut followed the line of Seni's arm. Yes! He saw the twinkling North Star.

"That is not the brightest star in the sky however. That honour goes to another constellation which is, at present, on the far side of what I call the Milky Way. The brightest star is known as Sirius, the dog star, because of the shape of the stars in that constellation or group."

"Tut and I were wondering about that part of the sky when we came up to have a look yesterday" said

Maya.

"I think of it as the Milky Way," said Seni, "because it looks as though the gods dropped a large container of milk which then spread out and covered the stars that were there. I have yet to learn all the mysteries of that part of the sky. My whole time is not devoted to the stars, I still have to carry out other duties within the temple," he said by way of explanation.

"If you look down towards the south-west of the North Star you will notice four stars. Imagine a line is drawn between each star and you will see it makes a box shape. Just a little way down from the 'box stars,'" said Seni, pointing north-easterly, "you can see another group of stars which loop around with a long handle. Can you see that, Prince?" asked Seni.

Maya took Tut's hand and moved it in the direction indicated and gradually Tut could indeed make out the group of stars as described. "That group is a separate constellation," said Seni. "Further up to the right there is another group of stars which look like a snake with its tail stuck in the air and its head up.

Seni found the look of wonder and excitement on Tut's face gratifying as the child recognised the patterns being described to him. When Seni saw recognition in Tut's countenance, he continued, "There are more stars in the sky than anyone can count and many, many groups of stars making up constellations. Some groups appear to be human in form while others are in the shape of animals. The problem with studying the sky is that not all stars stay in the same place. Some seem to move with the seasons.

"As well as setting the public calendar," continued Seni, "the Master Astronomers have worked out how to measure distances by using the stars. In Egypt, as you are no doubt aware Prince, we use the Royal Cubit which is made up of seven hands'-width. In field surveys the *meh-at* is equal to one hundred royal cubits. For larger areas the *setjat* is equal to one hundred cubits square. I must confess to not fully understanding how such matters are worked out since I still have much to learn."

"Looking up there convinces me of the existence of the gods," said Maya.

When the lesson was over Maya and Tut accompanied Seni to the front door where a servant was waiting with a bright torch. Seni could just make out the outline of his father, talking with the gatekeeper.

He bade them good night and followed the servant

to the gate. As he was leaving with his father, Seni looked back and saw Maya and Tut waving to him.

Seni came back at regular monthly intervals. Over time, when he began to feel comfortable in Maya and Tut's company, he explained that his father was a priest and he, as the eldest son, had to follow his father into the priesthood. He did not like all the rites and rituals that had to be learnt because, said Seni, "none of it stimulated my mind."

Since he had a natural love for the stars he worked in his spare time looking at the star maps in the House of Learning. After about a year of doing this he took courage and told his father he would prefer to be an astronomer priest. To his surprise his father arranged an interview for him with the High Priest. At that interview the High Priest was so impressed with the knowledge Seni had gleaned on his own, he agreed to appoint him apprentice to a Master Astronomer.

"I don't mean to sound boastful, Highness, it's my love of the subject that makes me sound so. I am now learning how to tell the time at night," said Seni. "The time is determined by listing the rising, cumulation and setting of various stars during thirty-six ten-day periods in the year. It is early days yet but once I understand it Prince, I will explain it to you."

"We do not think you boastful, Seni" said Maya. "Tut and I appreciate your feelings, it makes learning all the more enjoyable."

Tut had come to enjoy his time with Seni. He felt a comradeship towards him akin to that he felt for Nakht and his heart warmed towards Seni. At the end of one lesson soon after Tut's fifth birthday Seni asked to have a word alone with Maya. Maya asked Swnwt to get Tut ready for bed while she accompany Seni to the gate.

"I asked one of my friends studying astrology to do a reading for me. I gave him the Prince's details, date and time of birth without saying it was the Prince. The reading was not good. The Prince has powerful enemies. His very life is in the balance. The reading predicts him dying young yet, my friend says the Prince will be better known than any Pharaoh either before or after his reign."

Sensing Maya's distress, Seni added, "You must remember my friend is only a little older than I and he may have misread the signs but I thought it prudent to inform you."

"I am very glad that you did. Thank you, Seni, for not saying anything in front of the Prince. Good night."

It seems the stars do not lie, thought Maya as she

walked slowly towards the villa. Our Prince does indeed have enemies. Could my first instinct about Swnwt have been right after all? Is she spying for Tut's enemies? So difficult to tell. Tiya is taking precautions. I will have to take comfort from that, she thought.

Chapter 15

About fifteen days after Manetho's conversation with Tiya in the garden on the day of feeding the trees, the time came for Tut and Manetho to visit the stables. Both Tiya and Maya were anxious but realised they could not keep Tut in the house indefinitely. He had to face the dangers of life regardless of age, they agreed, or he would never learn to rule either himself or his country.

That morning Tut was dressed in plain garb, as was Manetho and his assistant. With Manetho on one side and the young, well-built gardener on the other side of Tut, the trio left the villa soon after sunrise.

Goatskin padding had been placed under the linen cloth to provide better protection for Tut's inner thighs while on the donkey. Tut's bow, arrows and boomerang were in a leather bag slung across his shoulder. Manetho had a heavy club on his left side and a thick stick on his right. The under gardener had a thick pole tied to his horse. They had the usual supply of water, dates, bread and cheese.

As the group left the safety of the villa Tiya sent up a silent prayer to Amun to keep her grandson's party safe.

Manetho kept to the main thoroughfare as much as possible. As they neared the last *fellahin* village before the open desert, large rocks lined either side of the path. Manetho whispered to the other two to be alert since this was the spot where a surprise attack could be launched. Manetho had his club ready. The young gardener untied his weapon.

As they rode towards the rocks they noticed what looked like a pile of old clothes lying in their path. Tut retrieved his bow and an arrow from his bag. As they reached the pile they could see it was a man. His face was in the sand. It was difficult to assess whether he was young or old.

Manetho, signalling Tut and the gardener to stay mounted, got off his horse and walked cautiously towards the prone body. With his club he prodded the man.

No sooner had he done so but there was a whooping and shouting and men came running from behind the rocks towards Tut. Manetho ran to protect the Prince. The young gardener was doing a good job with his long pole and even Tut was trying to take aim with his bow and arrow.

As Manetho was defending his charge he noted several other men joining in the mêlée but they seem to be attacking the attackers!

Manetho heard a loud shrill cry and looked over to Tut's donkey to see a man plunging a knife at the boy's heart. The impact knocked the child off the donkey and he landed on the sand, his body still.

Manetho, his heart pounding, filled with despair, attacked the assassin, clubbing him to death.

He then rushed to the Prince and turned him over gently. Strange, no blood. Manetho patted Tut's face gently. He had only fainted. On loosening his shirt Manetho saw Tut was wearing a fine close chain link vest. He heaved a sigh of relief, wiping the perspiration from his face with his sleeve. Whoever thought of that was to be thanked for saving Tut's life.

Tut was coming round. He looked up at Manetho, the child's eyes full of wonder.

"Manetho, when I fell it was like arms caught me and laid me gently on the sand. The only pain I have is across my chest where that man hit me."

Manetho realised all was quiet. He looked around and saw four dead men. He breathed out slowly as he realised the young gardener was not among the dead but was resting against a rock, his head in his hands.

"Are you able to continue, Prince?" asked Manetho as Tut finished the drink Manetho had offered him.

"Certainly," came the reply.

Manetho went over to the gardener. He had some bruising around his face and a large bump on the right side of his head but was otherwise alright. The young man told Manetho he saw three men make off as soon as the Prince sat up and spoke.

"Oh, my bow is broken!"

"Don't worry," laughed Manetho, with relief, as he went back to the Prince. "It's your birthday soon, I will make you another. I know just where to get the right wood for such a job. Come, we must continue our journey. Are you two up to it?"

Both Tut and the under gardener replied "Yes." When they reached the stables Manetho's friend led them to his private quarters to clean up and administer to their cuts and bruises. After the party had rested they were taken to see the horses. Manetho's friend explained to the Prince that he bred only Arabian horses because they were intelligent, beautiful, self-assured animals. Tut fell in love at once and forgot all about the attack. He chose a horse that was pure white. She seemed to recognise him and rubbed her delicate face against his ever so gently and whinnied as though she was greeting an old friend.

"What is her name?"

"Safia," replied Manetho's friend. "Good choice. She is young, fleet of foot and has an excellent temperament."

Manetho arranged for lessons to start after Tut's

fifth birthday. They had lunch and made their way back home in the cool of late afternoon.

Although they were vigilant, nothing untoward occurred on their homeward journey. On passing the place where the attack occurred they could see the vultures had been busy taking the meat off the bones of the bodies which were now giving off a strong stench. Manetho ensured he rode to the side of Tut so that, whilst the boy could smell the decaying bodies, he could not see them.

As the evening drew in neither Tiya nor Maya could eat or settle to anything. Both were sick with anxiety so much so that the servants could not help but feel their distress. Swnwt in particular wondered whether anything she had said in her report had caused Tut to be in danger. Tut being in danger, she reasoned, would be the only cause for such tension.

When the weary travellers entered the gates of the villa the whole household breathed a sigh of relief. Tut was lifted off his donkey and handed to Maya. The under-gardener took the animals while Manetho had a talk with Tiya, asking whether he could report to her after he had had a wash and change.

"Come and take supper with Maya and myself,"

replied Tiya noting the discolouration on the left side of Manetho's face and his bruised knuckles.

Maya's handmaiden Zelda, who also assisted in the care of Tut, had gone to get a bucket of warm water on Tut's arrival which was now in his bathroom. Maya took him into the bathroom, removed his clothing and the chain vest, checking his body for injuries.

"I am fine. Maya. It's just my chest." He pointed where the knife had been thrust. There was now a big black and blue bruise. Maya's eyes grew large with fear as she fought back the tears of anger that anyone should dare attack her boy.

She hugged him gently. "I thought I might lose you."

"Your chain vest saved me from the assassin's knife. Where did you get it?"

"It was a present from your father for your birthday last year. I put it away until I thought it might be needed."

"Why would anyone want me dead, Maya? I have asked this before but I cannot recall your answer."

"I am not sure, Tut. It must be some sort of power game. Someone does not want you to be pharaoh. I cannot think who that person might be though. Come on let us get you washed. Your evening meal is waiting. I ordered you some warm milk with bread and honey. Your favourite."

When Tut was in bed he remembered falling off the donkey and told Maya about it.

"You must have a god watching over you, or maybe your mother's spirit," she said. "If you were mine and the gods took me I would want my spirit to be close to you. Now rest and sleep."

That night Tut dreamt his mother catching him in her arms as he fell off his donkey.

After Tut had fallen asleep and Maya had safely hidden the chain vest, she went to Tiya's quarters to take supper with her. She had not realised, until now, how hungry she was.

Manetho was already there. The three tucked into boiled pigeon, wheat flavoured with mint, lightly fried vegetables and unleavened bread, all washed down with cool water for Maya and wine for the other two.

Having sated their hunger the three adjourned to the other side of the room, sinking into comfortable chairs. "Now Manetho, tell us everything that occurred from the time you left the villa," said Tiya.

Manetho related the ambush, explaining they were helped by some men who had seemed to come from nowhere and disappeared after the fight. "That chain vest saved the Prince's life. Whose idea was that?" He looked at Tiya who in turn looked at Maya.

"It was a gift from his father. It seemed the time to put it to use," replied Maya.

"The only explanation," said Tiya, "is that my son had a small band of soldiers watching over his son."

"Do you think he knows about the visits to Karnak?" asked Manetho.

"I don't think so or I would have heard from him about it by now," replied Tiya. "He must have discovered a plot and taken protective steps. In light of this event we will keep Tut's birthday a quiet family gathering as usual."

All three were having trouble stifling their yawns. So they bade each other "Good night".

That night Captain Djer reported the events of the day to the King. They had captured one of the attackers but he was unable to give any information as to who instructed the attack. He was just asked, he had said, to play dead in order to stop the travellers. The men who actually carried out the attack were killed.

"What shall we do with the prisoner, Highness?"

"Let him go but keep him under surveillance for

the next ten days and let me know if he meets anyone from the palace. And I mean anyone. You are certain my son is safe? Where were they travelling to?"

"Yes, Highness. We were discreet and watched over the group until they reached the stables in the Eastern Desert. The Prince was talking and seemed happy. I got close enough to see him choose a beautiful white horse. We did not leave them until they were safely back at the villa."

"I see my mother takes her role as King-Maker seriously," mused the Pharaoh.

Chapter 16

As soon as Maya took Tut into the bathroom Swnwt appeared and said to Zelda that she, Swnwt, would assist Maya in putting Tut to bed. Zelda thanked her and left. Swnwt immediately tiptoed to the bathroom door just in time to hear Tut relate being hit by the assassin's knife and landing gently on the sand. Swnwt had to put her hand over her mouth to stop herself exclaiming. She was happy Tut was unhurt but now she was fearful for her own safety. Swnwt moved away from the door as Maya started to wash Tut. She prepared his bed, laid out a clean vest and night shift and left.

After the three adults had finished supper and the servants had cleared away, no one noticed Swnwt creep behind the open door leading to Tiya sitting area. She needed more information about the attack in order to make a full report to the Queen. She tiptoed away as soon as Manetho finished his report and, fortunately, before he mentioned the Karnak visits.

Before long it was time for Swnwt to make her monthly visit to her mother. "Why are you looking so anxious?" asked Maya as she saw Swnwt leaving.

"No reason. Well… my mother has been talking about finding me a husband and I do not want to get married. I enjoy my work and my life here. I do not feel the need, at present, for any more than that" replied Swnwt with a wry smile.

"I never knew my mother." This came out of Maya's mouth before she realised. It was not like her to give information about herself, least of all to someone who might be a spy.

Yet the effect on Swnwt was profound. She felt bad lying to Maya and now she felt worse but she could see no way out of her predicament. She had not asked to become a spy and was not in a position to refuse when commandeered. She smiled at Maya. "I am sorry you never knew your mother but that could be seen as a blessing since you were able to be there for Lady Kiya and the Prince. I must leave now," said Swnwt as she dashed out of the villa.

As usual, before seeing her mother, Swnwt reported to the Queen's head housekeeper. She related what she knew of the attack on Tut and the mysterious men who assisted in fighting off the attackers.

"Polydama," said Swnwt, "can you ask for me to be released from my duty to report on the Prince's household? They are becoming suspicious of me since the attack. I can see it in the Lady Tiya's eyes."

"I doubt the Queen will release you but I will ask if

opportunity arises."

Poly felt a twinge of pity for the young woman and a little guilty that it was she who had put Swnwt's name forward.

"Are you afraid of the Queen? asked Swnwt.

"Sometimes, if truth be told. I have been with her since she was fifteen, when she married Pharaoh Akhenaten. I know her moods and how to pacify her but I would never presume to understand, or underestimate her."

"How is it you have survived so long in her service and she places such trust in you?" continued Swnwt.

"I find her mesmerising. She has always been confident and sure of what she wants. I could not disobey her even if I wanted to. I am completely under her spell. I both fear and adore her."

"But why?" insisted Swnwt.

"Because she deigned to look upon me kindly and agree to my being her handmaiden when others spat at me, called me too ugly to have around. This ravishingly beautiful young woman chose me for her personal body servant. I would follow her into the fires of hell and that feeling has only grown over time."

"You are not ugly!"

"She taught me how to make the most of the little

the gods blessed me with. Kohl make my eyes less round. Copying her diet has helped me to be less ungainly and taking her lead in colours I wear all enhance my poor looks."

"Poly, we have a spy in our midst," said the Queen on receiving the report. Those men could only have been from the King's private guards. Find that spy, Poly. I don't care what you have to do but find her. Start by finding out where all the female servants who work in my apartments were when we had our conversation that day."

Before long word reached Kara, through gossip, that the Queen's housekeeper was looking for a spy in the Queen's household and that all her servants were being questioned. Kara could not imagine what punishment the Queen would inflict on the perpetrator but she suspected it would involve an early grave.

None of the servants knew what had become of the midwife who delivered the young Prince. She had disappeared without trace within a week of his birth. Most believe she became food for worms on the Queen's orders.

Kara managed to get a coded message to the King by way of one of his designated private guards. The following day she received word back to be ready to leave the Palace that evening. The person coming to meet her would use the code word "Celestial" so she would know he came from the King. The message went on to inform her that arrangements had been made for her to marry a trusted courtier who admired her and had asked the King, some time ago, to have her for his wife. She was to be taken to the courtier's family home in Thebes until her marriage. Being under the King's protection would ensure she was well-treated.

Kara was bemused to learn she had an admirer and that he wanted to marry her. She had very little to pack so she left everything as it was in her room and went about her duties as usual.

When she got to the kitchen of the Queen's quarters Poly was waiting for her.

"After breakfast come and see me before your start your duties," said Poly. Kara inclined her head in the affirmative. She had to make a concerted effort to appear unconcerned at the summons and made herself have her usual bowl of porridge.

She went to the head housekeeper's office, knocked and was told to "Come in."

"Tell me," said Poly, "can you recollect where you

were on this day fourteen days ago?"

Kara cast her mind back. "Yes" she said "I was not well and was in my room. Do you remember sending the kitchen maid to look for me?"

"I was told you came down to breakfast that morning as usual and after, you went to collect the clean laundry," replied Poly.

"I did start to go to the laundry room but my women's problem started early. I had to rush to my room. I did not want to cause a mess or faint on duty. I was not well enough to look for you."

Poly gave the girl a penetrating look before saying, "That will be all for now but I may need to speak with you again." The girl seemed nervous but then all the maids were when they entered her office, she reasoned.

Kara was shaking once she left the office. Maybe, she thought, it is time to leave. Although the thought of marriage terrified her, she decided to trust the King's judgment. He had always been kind to her even when she was a child.

She suspected she was his child. Her mother had been a beauty in her time. She had been given a small villa in Memphis, for services to the Crown, while Kara was kept at court and trained to be a maid. By the age of sixteen she had only seen her mother a few times a year, on high days and holidays. Since the court moved to Akhenhaten she had not seen her mother at all.

The King being her father would explain his interest in her and his desire to see her safe. She decided to suppress her fears and get through the day as best she could.

In the retired servants' quarters of the palace, Swnwt was talking with her mother who had been given certain privileges as a result of her daughter's usefulness to the Queen. She had been moved to larger rooms, well-furnished for a retired servant's quarters; with its own bathroom and a handmaiden to assist her.

Swnwt explained to her mother the difficulty she was in because the Queen insisted on her spying on the Prince's household and the situation leading to them becoming suspicious of her.

"There is little you can do, my child" said her mother. "We are allowed no free will. We are owned by our masters and I do not want to see you harmed. All l can advise is that you continue as you have been for the past five years. It is a question of survival. I could give up this pleasant life but where would we go? How would two lone women survive in this land? Also, we would never be free of the Queen's wrath if you left your post."

"Maybe you are right, Mother. We are like flies caught in a spider's web."

The two women hugged. It was time for Swnwt to return to the villa.

Chapter 17

Tut woke early on the morning of his fifth birthday. He could not wait for the day to begin. Maya cautioned him to slow down or he would be too tired when his father arrived. She gave him the present she had for him, a well-made multi-coloured hat of leather, lined with fine red linen. It fitted well but made him seem older than he was.

"Is this why you needed to measure my head?" he laughed. "So it was nothing to do with how clever I might be?"

She had ordered his favourite dishes for breakfast. Delicately flavoured calf's kidneys; fresh bread and honey, sycamore dates and a small glass of pomegranate wine allowed only on his birthday. She had porridge.

After breakfast she left the maids to clear up and followed the excited boy down the stairs to see his Nana. Tiya was just finishing her breakfast of porridge and a piece of bread and honey when Tut bounded into her quarters, waving his new hat. He allowed his Nana to give him a hug and kiss on each cheek.

"Would you like to see what I have got you now or later?" teased his Nana.

"Now, now, now, Nana!"

She got out a highly polished box from the cupboard to the side of her.

"What is it Nana?"

"Open it and have a look. Gently now."

Tut inspected the box, found a metal clip, undid it and lifted the lid. There in front of him was an array of different-coloured paints in small containers with different size brushes made from horse hair attached to smooth wooden handles. There was one container with nothing in it.

"What should be in this one, Nana?"

"That is to put water in to mix the colours. I also have a pile of papyrus for you to paint on. You will have to do me a painting of your new hat."

"Thank you, Nana. I love painting and will very much enjoy using your present." With that he threw his arms around her neck. "I will have to show this to Swnwt," he said.

Just then there was a knock on Tiya's door. Maya opened it. It was Manetho. "May I come in and wish the Prince many happy returns?" Manetho had his hands behind his back. Maya moved aside to let him in. Tut turned to him with an expectant look.

"Can you think what I may have for you?" he asked Tut.

"I am very much hoping you have made me a

bow."

"Yes. You are right. I have made it bigger than your other one and I have engraved your throne name as on the original your father gave you," he replied as he brought the bow from behind his back.

"Ooh!" said Tut. "I will have to learn to handle this new bow. I wish Nakht was here," he said wistfully.

"I miss him. He taught me to shoot, to use the boomerang, to swim in the Nile and to hunt for birds' feathers."

"To swim in the Nile?" repeated his Nana, looking at Maya questioningly.

"I will explain later," promised Maya. "I have to check on the activities in the kitchen." As she rushed out of the room she noted Tut's apologetic look and smiled at him reassuringly.

The kitchen was busy preparing food for the royal guests and household. No children had been invited but the King had insisted that an entertainer be engaged.

The entertainer was due to arrive mid-morning. The King was expected when the sun was in the centre of the sky.

Tiya had agreed the servants' children could watch the show from a distance. Maya had ordered a small tent to be set up in the garden for the entertainer's use, with a table on which was a jar of pomegranate juice, a glass, a small mirror and a chair. He arrived earlier than expected, introduced himself to Maya and, with a dour look, went into the tent. As he put on his costume and then his makeup he scowled at the mirror.

"What am I, an entertainer to kings and princes, doing here at a villa of some unknown? Why was I commissioned by the King's own Head of Palace Entertainment to come and perform for some spoilt grandchild?"

It dawned to him that the grandparent must have influence at court. It would not do, he decided, to displease his superiors and thereby jeopardise his livelihood.

Sometime later he came out dressed in a brightly-coloured costume, his face painted with a big red smile, eyes looking large with kohl and bright green, oversized, wooden shoes to match his outfit. He walked as though he had two left feet which got Tut and the other children giggling before he had done anything.

Tut was sitting beside his Nana on an ornate golden chair made comfortable with colourful cushions embroidered with white, green, red and gold

Nile lilies.

The entertainer did not speak but used his face and hands to express what he was doing. His face seemed to light up as he set eyes on Tut and his Nana. He fell over his oversized shoes a few times which the adults found disconcerting but the children thought very funny. He pulled out three coloured balls from each pocket and started juggling which went down very well. He touched the Prince behind his left ear, having looked at Tiya for permission, and produced a tiny egg which he placed in front of Tut. He did the same from Tut's right ear. He then took both eggs in one hand, clapped his hands together and held them up. They were clean, no sign of the eggs. He then took a square piece of bright orange cloth from his shirt pocket. He shook it to show there was nothing in it. He then put his hands together round the cloth and when he opened his palms there were two small, beautiful, coloured birds which began to chirp.

Tut and the other children went wild with excitement. The entertainer let Tut touch the birds to satisfy himself they were real. He then closed his hands gently, moved them about a bit, clapped his hands again and *whoosh*, the birds were gone and only the orange cloth remained. The servants children clapped and clapped. Even Tut joined in.

After the show Maya, pleased to see the chap smiling, paid the entertainer with a big basket of bread, cheese, honey, fruits and vegetables from their garden and two bottles of home brewed beer. She also ensured he was provided with a meal.

Not long after the entertainer had left the King arrived with his Elite Guards and servants. Tut, pleased to see his father, told him all about the entertainment yet he did not hug or kiss his father until he was prompted to by his Nana. His father noted this and, while he understood that he was a near stranger in his son's life, it hurt him more deeply than he cared to show.

The King walked from the gates of the villa holding his son's hand and when they were in the reception area he sat, placing Tut on his lap.

"Well, my son, another year and you start training in earnest for taking your place as Pharaoh one day. You had a cousin, Smenkhare was his name. He would have inherited my throne but he died some time ago.

"What was he like, Father?"

He lived to be a grown man but, unlike you, he was always of a delicate constitution. He caught a chill, which led to a violent cough.

"The doctors tried but could not save him. He was the son of my older brother Tutmosis who also died young. It made the loss of Smen even harder to bear." The King paused, as though reminiscing, then visibly pulled himself back to the present.

"Would you like to see what I have brought for you?"

"Yes Father, I would," said Tut, getting excited again.

One of the courtiers brought forward a leather bag from which he took out a box. This one was inlaid with semi-precious stones and glittered in the sunlight. Tut, still sitting on his father's lap, took the box and opened it. There, inside, were rings of various sizes and designs, amulets on black cord and other pieces of jewellery but the item that caught Tut's attention was the broad collar necklace. Its falcon-headed terminals were inlaid with lapis lazuli, quartz, green felspar, obsidian and coloured glass. Over the collar was hung a separate necklace of three strands with lotus flowers and serpent terminals, signifying power.

"Father, is it true little people called dwarfs are used to make *Wesekh*, broad collars?"

"Who told you that?" laughed the King. It was the first time Tut had heard his father laugh. "Yes, it is true, dwarfs appear to have a special gift for this work. I have seen, in my youth, two dwarfs sitting opposite each other at a low table working together stringing and arranging the beads and tying off the threads. Other workers hold the strings between the soles of their feet and twist with their palms but dwarfs sit face to face holding the end of a string taut while the other splices its two strands together."

Tiya was smiling. This was the longest conversation father and son had enjoyed together. Maya put the presents the King had brought in a safe place.

It was time for the mid-day meal and as usual Tiya's cooks had excelled themselves. There was a wonderful assortment of roasted meats, vegetables seasoned with coriander, cumin, mustard and thyme. Sweetmeats, sultanas, figs and cinnamon cakes. Beer for the King, wine for the adults and pomegranate juice for Maya and Tut.

The meal was just coming to an end when a tall, bronze, clean-shaven, well-built young man entered the room. He bowed to Tiya and the King, apologising for the intrusion. Tut suddenly realised who it was. He jumped out of his seat shouting, "Nakht, you are back!" He threw his arms round Nakht's legs.

Nakht picked Tut up and twirled him round.

"May we have leave, Highness?" The King nodded and Nakht, carrying Tut, with Maya following, left the room and went into the garden.

Maya noticed Nakht's hair was close cropped and he had a couple of new colourful feathers attached to the back of his head which Tut had also only just noticed.

The King was surprised to feel a stab of pain in his chest at witnessing the rapturous welcome Tut bestowed on Nakht. His mother noted the fleeting look of anguish on her son's face.

"Nakht is a member of your military, just come back from quelling the Nubian uprising. He used to come here most weeks to teach Tut how to use the bow and arrow. They use to wrestle and play-fight together. I thought it good for the boy to have male company," explained his mother.

"A good thought, Mother. He is an able young man, an outstanding soldier."

"My son, something is puzzling me. I wonder whether you can assist."

The King looked at his mother affectionately. "Speak."

"I did not tell you about the recent attack made on Tut's life because you already have so much to deal with. Yet I suspect you know of it. Was it your soldiers, in disguise, that came to Tut's aid?"

"Yes. You will not be surprised to hear that I have ways of finding out what is going on, especially where the welfare of the future king is concerned. We caught one of the men alive but got no leads as to who instigated the attack."

"Would I be right in thinking the order came from the Queen?"

Her son's face clouded over. "That is not a matter for discussion, Mother."

"Forgive me. I should have known better. Do not be angry. I see you so rarely. It was a thoughtless question. Say you forgive me."

"There is nothing to forgive, Mother. You are a woman and must have your say. I am not angry. Let us part friends."

As was his habit, he kissed his mother on each hand. They walked out of the villa and into the garden where Tut and Maya were listening to Nakht talk about the feathers he was wearing.

The conversation stopped as the King, Tiya and the King's retinue came down the steps of the villa. Maya gave Tut a gentle push towards his father.

"Thank you father for coming to my birthday celebration and for the fine presents you have given me." Tut saw something in his father's face which encouraged him to go up to his father, put his arms around his waist, his head against his father's flesh and give his father a hug. The King patted his son on the head and left smiling.

Tiya went in to rest. Nakht showed Tut the correct way to hold the bow he received from Manetho. The three sat by the pond watching the changing colours of the water as the sunlight hit the falling drops from the spouting fountain.

"Would you like to see what I brought back for you, Prince?"

"You brought something for me from Nubia?"

Nakht delved into the leather bag, which had been slung across his shoulder, and brought out five very fine, colourful bird feathers.

"I assumed you would like these. Don't ask me which native Nubian birds they come from. We moved from place to place often and I cannot now recollect their names."

"They are wonderful. I shall enjoy wearing them. What else did you get whilst fighting?" asked Tut.

"Some scars." Nakht showed them the long, still angry looking, scar on his right thigh and a few less conspicuous ones on both arms. "I wore light armour, made of tough leather, which protected the vital organs of my body. I have something else to show you."

Nakht dug into the leather bag again and pulled out a shiny medal. On it was written "Gold of Bravery".

"What did you have to do to earn that?" asked Maya, who was trying not to stare longingly at Nakht while he talked with Tut.

Nakht's body had filled out, become more masculine - no trace remained of the boy she first met five years previously. She was surprised at the hunger she felt as she noted his rippling chest muscles and firm muscular thighs. He had an aura of strength and easy confidence which made her feel weak with desire. She wanted to caress that body, to feel its warmth against her. Maya, shocked at her thoughts made a supreme effort to clear her mind and remember she had dedicated her life to Tut and there was no room for a lover, however desirable.

"It's an award for valour on the field of battle. Horemheb himself awarded it to me. I am the youngest officer to receive this medal." Nakht could not disguise the note of pride in his voice. "My mother has not seen it yet." He looked at Maya as he said this. Maya pretended not to understand the significance of Nakht's remark. "I came straight here to wish you happy birthday, Prince."

"I understood you were going to be away for longer," said Maya.

"So did I before we left but the uprising was easy enough to quell. Time was taken in collecting the outstanding taxes."

Tut wanted to hear what Nakht had actually done to earn the medal but Maya intervened.

"That is enough for now. Its time you were abed. It's been a long day. Nakht, can you have a word with Manetho? Tut will be starting horse riding lessons in six days and it would help if you could be there."

"I will see him now if he is available. Goodnight Prince" said Nakht, bending down to be at eye level. "I will see you soon." Tut flung his arms round Nakht's neck and held on as though he would not let go.

Maya gave Nakht a warm smile as she prised Tut away from him. "It's so good to have you back in one piece. Goodnight." She whirled the Prince round and the two walked into the villa. Nakht, swallowing his disappointment at Maya's cool reception, went to find Manetho.

Manetho was at the back sorting out and putting away the gardening tools he had been cleaning all afternoon. The two men hailed each other as trusted friends.

"You have matured since we last met, if I am not mistaken," said Manetho.

"A few battle scars does that to a man" responded Nakht. "Maya tells me you will be taking Tut to horse riding lessons. She thought I may be of service."

"The Prince and I were attacked on our first visit to the Stables which is in the Eastern Desert. I had one of the under-gardeners with me and he fought well enough. However, I am not at ease with putting a young untrained man in peril. Having a trained fighting man along would go some way to easing the Lady Tiya's and Maya's concern for Tut's safety.

"I understand," replied Nakht.

The two discussed Nakht's availability and made arrangements accordingly.

Nakht collected his horse and made his way back to his barracks in a thoughtful frame of mind. He had hoped his absence would have softened Maya's heart towards him, yet there had been no evidence of it when he had entered the villa nor when they were in the garden with Tut. Well, she may love me as a brother but I know she adores Tut. I must continue to help keep him safe. Maybe, over time, I will win her heart that way.

Chapter 18

Poly had interviewed all the maids and servants yet not one appeared to have been in the vicinity when she had the conversation with the Queen about the Prince.

On the day following her questioning of Kara it was reported to Poly that Kara had not come to the kitchen at her usual time for breakfast. The cook had sent one of the kitchen maids to see whether Kara was ill. She found the room empty and the bed not slept in.

The only conclusion Poly could come to was that Kara was the spy. Poly was fearful of the Queen's reaction to the news that the culprit had flown. She said a prayer to the gods and decided to wait until after the mid-day meal to inform the Queen. She went to see the Cook to order the preparation of one of the Queen's favourite dishes for lunch, pigeon stuffed with mint and herbs with fresh berries to follow. That should put her in a pleasant mood, thought Poly.

Poly then made enquiry of all her sources within the Palace to ascertain when and where Kara may have gone. Kara seemed to have vanished. As a last resort Poly visited the stables, taking with her some freshly made cinnamon buns. She saw a couple of stable boys mucking out the stalls. The gods were on her side, one of them was her nephew.

"Hello nephew. I have two fresh cinnamon buns here. Would you and your friend like one?" This was an unusual occurrence.

"Hello Aunt Poly. I have not seen you here at this time of day before."

"I just thought you could do with a treat." The look and smell of the buns won the day. Both boys took the offered treat and bit into it with relish.

"Thank you Auntie."

"How many horses do you look after between you?" Poly asked. She continued to make conversation asking, in a caring tone, how long their day was and whether the stable master was a good man to work for.

Noting they had relaxed Poly then asked "Were any horses taken out in the night?" Her nephew replied, "Yes, two horses and a small coach."

"Who took them?"

"One of the King's courtiers. I heard him saying he had to visit his mother urgently."

"Did he have anyone with him?"

"Funny that. Yes, a young woman who seemed very shy. Kept her face covered."

"I am glad you enjoyed the buns. I had better let

you two get back to work," said Poly.

"Thank you for the bun Auntie."

"Yes. Thank you" said the other boy.

When Poly was out of earshot the younger boy stopped raking out and said, "I wonder what all that was about. I hope we did not do wrong answering her questions."

Poly's nephew looked at him and shrugged. "My Aunt Poly works for the Queen so I can't see how we can get into trouble for speaking with her."

Poly felt better as she returned to the Queen's quarters. Since no one else was missing from the household and there were currently no female guests, Poly decided it had to be Kara - and the King - was involved.

Poly went to her room, washed her hands and face and changed her clothes and shoes, which smelt of horse manure. The Queen would have had her meal by now, thought Poly as she left the safety of her own sanctum.

It was a hot afternoon. The Queen was on her chaise on the balcony enjoying the breeze. "Ah, Poly. What news of our betrayer?"

"Highness, my investigations lead me to believe

our spy was Kara, the maid who was responsible for linen and towels."

"How can you be so certain?"

Poly reported her questioning of the maids, the events of the morning, finding Kara gone and her conversation with the stable boys who confirmed one of the King's courtiers left in the night with a woman.

The Queen's eyes narrowed. So the girl was spying for Aten. What made him trust her? she wondered.

She never paid any attention to the girl, why should she have? Yet, on reflection, as Kara had become a young woman her looks had reminded the Queen of a woman who had been a servant in the palace many years ago. She only remembered the woman because one day she happened to notice the King looking at her with that particular light in his eyes which she, the Queen, thought was reserved only for her. She had the woman moved to the kitchens but had no idea what became of her.

Poly was not sure whether to leave. The Queen had not said a word since Poly had finished her report. She decided to give a little cough. The Queen looked up, startled.

"Poly! You may go." Poly bowed and beat a hasty retreat, pleased that her timing had worked in her favour.

The Queen remained deep in thought. Should she confront the King? Indeed, what could she say? He obviously knew she had had a hand in the latest attack on the Prince's life. Yet he had said nothing. If she mentioned the girl it could cause a rift between them which would serve no purpose. Best to leave matters as they are and say nothing. She decided all her new maids in future would have to be more carefully vetted.

That evening Nefertiti took particular care with her toilet. She had her handmaiden anoint her body with essence of jasmine. She wore a fine, loose yellow linen gown which showed her sensual body to advantage. She looked and smelt seductive.

When the King came to her chamber that evening his eyes lit up at the sight of her. He put all his cares out of his mind and allowed himself to be loved in a way only this woman, his Queen, could love and satisfy him.

He could not explain, even to himself, the sway she had over him or how he could so easily overlook her efforts to destroy his only male child. All he knew was they shared a passion for each other that defied understanding.

Chapter 19

When Swnwt returned from visiting her mother she told Maya that the Prince's step-sister, Meretaten was with child but was very ill. Maya mentioned this to Tiya who was concerned to find out more.

"Maya, although I have not had the opportunity to know my granddaughters I love them dearly. They are the children of my child, how can I feel otherwise? I will write to my son asking whether he will agree to me coming to see my sick grandchild. I could help by spending time with her."

The letter was sent the very next day. Manetho was entrusted with the task of delivering it and awaiting a reply. He returned late the same day with a letter in the King's own hand.

The King stated that whilst he could not see how his mother's visit would help he had no objection to her wanting to spend time with her granddaughter and would ensure rooms were prepared in close proximity to Meretaten's.

"Maya, do you realise I have never stayed at my son's Palace before? Yet I feel compelled to see my first grandchild in her hour of need."

Tiya, in preparation for her departure, showed Maya where the housekeeping funds were kept; who needed to be paid when and how much. The household accounts were also handed over to her.

"I have no concerns about leaving you in charge, Maya."

"Tiya, your aged handmaiden, Edfu, is not very good on her feet. I would feel happier if my handmaiden Zelda accompanied you also. She knows how the palace works and can do any running around needed. Swnwt and I can manage here. Please do not over tire yourself. Remember, Tut and I need you too."

"Don't mention illness to Tut, Maya. I will say I am visiting the palace for a change of air. There is no need to worry the child."

Manetho arranged for a carriage to take Tiya and her ladies to the palace. Tut was not happy at the prospect of his Nana leaving. He had never been away from her for more than a day in his life. Not knowing when she was to return was also distressing him. Tiya's heart melted at the look of anxiety on her grandson's face.

"You know I would not leave you unless it was really important. You have to trust me when I say I will come back. Be good and do your lessons. I want to hear about all your adventures when I get back. Use that birthday present I gave you to paint me a picture of the garden. Maya will look after you as she always has. Now smile for me."

Tut made a pathetic attempt at a smile.

On reaching the palace Tiya and her ladies were taken to a suite of rooms to the rear of the building, with views over the flower gardens. There were five rooms in the suite: three bedrooms, each one with its own adjoining bathroom; a dining area and a large reception room, which was well-furnished with chairs covered in sumptuous cushions; a chaise for Tiya to rest on, and alabaster lamps decorated with colourful lotus flowers were placed around the rooms to ensure they were well lit at night.

Tiya's bedroom was a little smaller than the one she occupied at her villa but it was comfortable. The bed was placed against the south wall of the room; ornate carved boxes for clothing were against the wall nearest the bathroom. There was a beautiful small table near the bed, inlaid with coloured glass. The lamps were already prepared for the evening with sesame oil and fresh floating wicks.

The bathroom was spacious with a large mirror placed so as to reflect the light from the high wall opening. She especially liked the polished wooden seat over the sand bucket. There were stools scattered about in case she needed to sit while being washed.

While Tiya was in the bathroom freshening up Maya's maid Zelda emptied Tiya's bags, putting her creams, ointments, comb and makeup on the tall table, a jug of water and glass on the small inlaid table and her clothes in the storage boxes provided.

Zelda was a quiet, plain-looking girl of about twenty with lack lustre brown hair and dull grey eyes. When she was assigned to Maya on Princess Kiya's arrival at the palace, the girl's eyes had had a vacant look. Maya, through kindness and patience, had done a good job of bringing Zelda out of herself, training her to be thorough and to take pride in her work.

Maya discovered Zelda had been brought back as a slave from an Asiatic campaign. It was believed she became the way she was after seeing her parents beheaded in front of her and her village razed to the ground. Some described her as simple but Maya was fiercely protective of the young woman, firmly believing there was a good brain in a head that only displayed, as yet, fear and timidity. The attack on Baby Tut that Zelda witnessed had set her back but, five years on, she was becoming more confident.

Tiya's old maid, who had been in her employ since Tiya left her father's home as a bride, was resting. The jostling of the carriage had rattled all her bones, she informed Zelda.

"My dear," said Tiya as she came back into the bedroom, "What is your name?"

Zelda turned red in the face. She was not used to being spoken to by Tiya.

She gulped and told Tiya her name.

"That is an unusual name."

"I am told I was born in Asia and brought to Egypt by soldiers."

"Zelda, can you find your way to my sick granddaughter's apartment. It should be nearby, and ask when I might see her.

Zelda realised she would have to be brave. Maya was not here to help her and no Swnwt to hide behind. She felt really exposed but not wanting to let Maya down she resolved to find the courage needed to do her mistress's bidding. Zelda returned and reported to Tiya that the King's physician was with the princess.

"Please take me there. I want to speak with the physician."

They hurried along the corridor they had come down earlier and turned right into a wider corridor. Just as Tiya and Zelda walked into the vestibule the doctor was coming out of a door on the far side.

As he came towards her Tiya raised her right hand,

dismissing Zelda, who retreated into the corridor.

"Doctor, I am Meretaten's grandmother. Could we sit down a minute, I really want to understand what is wrong with her."

The tall well-built man with a pleasing face except for the permanent frown, looked at Tiya intently and his face broke into a smile.

"You probably do not remember me. I was a child in Pharaoh Amenhotep III court. My father was court physician and he sometimes let me accompany him. You were always kind to me."

"I do remember you. You were a well- behaved child but, forgive me, I cannot recollect your name."

"Ir-en-Okhty. My father named me after a previous famous court physician. Do call me Ir-en. Let us sit down. You must be tired after your journey. The King mentioned to me that you were arriving today. You look younger than I expected."

The colour in Tiya's cheeks heightened at the compliment. "It is kind of you to say so although I do not feel young. Now please explain to me my granddaughter's malady."

The smile disappeared and the frown became pronounced. "The Princess is two hundred and ten days into her pregnancy. Her constitution has never been strong. She has had problems from the outset.

Severe sickness for the first thirty days. She could keep nothing down. As that passed she found it difficult to digest food. I recommended pulses, fresh fruit, vegetables, plenty of goat's milk and soft cheese. Yet her condition did not improve. She has been bed ridden for some one hundred and twenty days now. I have advised her that fresh air is important to her recovery but she simply does not have the energy to step out of the palace.

"There are further complications with the unborn child. I suspect it is malformed. The shape of her belly is wrong. There appears to be no arms or legs."

"Where is her husband?" asked Tiya.

"The child is her father's."

"Does he know the child may be malformed?"

"Yes."

"What does he suggest?"

"I have advised, in order to bring her suffering to an end, that I operate on the Princess and remove the child. In any event the Princess is far too weak to survive a natural birth. It is the only hope of saving her life."

"So why is that not being done?"

"The Princess will not agree. She says it will displease the gods and she will not be admitted to Abydos to be near Osiris when she dies."

"Unlike her father, she has not given up the old gods," murmured Tiya. "What can we do?"

"Keep her as comfortable as possible and let nature take its course. Her body has swollen - her face, her arms and legs. I suspect her body is poisoning itself. She is not drinking enough so the poison is getting stronger each day. It is a terrible trial for a doctor to watch a patient die but the Princess has tied my hands and the King will not go against her wishes."

"What about her mother? What does she say?"

"The Queen cannot bear to see her daughter's suffering. She receives daily reports."

"Ir-en, I have no wish to add to your burden. Can I help and if so how?"

"You can sit with her and hold her hand. Talk to her about times gone by, distract her. Encourage her to drink, feed her as you would a babe. She will not accept that from a servant but may from you."

"I will do all I can. May I go in now and see her for a few minutes?"

"Surely. I must go to the King. I will inform him of your arrival. He has been in conference all day with his deputy Ay and Horemheb his military leader. I will take my leave now but will look in on the Princess later this evening."

After a day of archery practice, wrestling, cloud gazing and general fooling around, Nakht and Tut were joined by Maya for a meal in the garden. Maya asked Nakht to tell them something about his family.

"You have never told us anything about yourself," she said.

"There is not much to tell. My father, Merenuka, is a priest and a relative of Ay the vizier; they are cousins, I think. My father never talks about his relations. The change of religion did not affect my father because he is the Chief Embalmer to the court. He prepared the old King's body and carried out all the rites for the dead on the King's behalf. He is also a priest in a private temple to Amun on the estate of a powerful nobleman whom the Pharaoh could not afford to have as an enemy.

"What is your mother like?" asked Maya.

"My mother, Damna, was a weaver in a workshop at the same temple as my father. That is how they met. She worked until she had my brother Hery-Shef. After that she weaved from home. Then I came along. She still harbours a desire to run her own weaving business but my father will not agree to his wife working outside the home even though he spends more time in the embalming chambers at the temple than at home."

"When did you join the army?"

"At the age of fourteen I obtained my father's permission to join the military. My mother was unhappy with my choice. She dotes on me and suffers greatly at the thought of me being killed or injured. I suspect she is lonely in that big empty house with only servants for company. I try to visit as often as I can but she wants daughters-in-law and grandchildren to fill her life. My brother has now worked his way up in the priesthood and at twenty three is looking for a suitable wife. I am hoping he finds one that will allow my mother to spoil her."

Maya looked at Nakht, her eyes soft, glowing. "I sympathise with your mother. I feel the same about Tut."

The child had laid his head on Maya's lap and was now fast asleep.

"You have worn him out."

Nakht picked Tut up gently in his strong arms and carried him up the stairs to his room with Maya following.

Chapter 20

As Tiya was about to enter Meretaten's bed chamber she recollected she had never met the girl. Blood will recognise blood, she decided. Making an effort to arrange her face into a relaxed smile, Tiya entered the room.

The sumptuousness of the décor took her breath away. It's been a long time since I was in such surroundings, she thought. The furniture and ornaments were azure-blue and gold. The walls were decorated with rich blue brocade interwoven with gold threads. The bed cover was in contrast a deep red with gold and silver hand stitched Nile lilies. The only splash of white was the fine linen curtains hanging over the open windows, moving gently in the breeze.

Tiya's eyes gradually returned to the bed where, hardly noticeable for the richness of the cushions and covering, lay the Princess. Her eyes were closed. Tiya walked quietly to the bed and sat on the chair placed close by it. Meretaten was actually on top of the red cover with a thin red linen sheet over her. The girl's face was puffy and bluish. Her arms and legs were covered. Tiya could make out the bump of her belly and could now see what the doctor meant. It was not the usual shape, neither standing proud of her body nor low slung.

Tiya leaned forward, put her hands under the thin cover and touched the girl's arm. Her skin was cool but felt unnaturally soft.

The young woman opened her eyes and looked questioningly at Tiya who smiled and said in a gentle but clear voice, "Hello my dear. I am your father's mother, your Nana. I heard you were ill and had to come and see you. In fact, if you will let me, I would like to stay with you until you are well again."

Meretaten gave her grandmother a wan smile. "My sisters Nefernaten and Ankhasenpaaten told me about you. They met you when they accompanied our father to our brother's birthday." She stopped to catch her breath.

Tiya looked around and saw an earthenware jug and goblet. She poured a drink and held it to Meretaten's mouth, putting her left hand, behind her granddaughter's head for support. The girl took the smallest of sips.

"Is there anything you really feel you would like to eat?" asked Tiya. "I brought some sycamore dates, some grapes and some honey with me. Can I tempt you with the grapes?" Meretaten opened her eyes again and smiled. "You are kind."

"That's what Nanas are for. It would give me pleasure to see you eat something."

"Some grapes would be welcome but I cannot swallow the skin."

"That is alright. I will have them peeled and sliced so it's easier for your body to absorb."

Tiya rang the bell which was on the bed beside Meretaten and gave her request. While they were waiting Tiya smoothed Meretaten's lank hair more to comfort herself than anything else. She hummed a lullaby she used to sing to her sons when they were young. She could not remember the words, only the tune.

Tiya managed to get Meretaten to eat three grapes. She could sense the shadow of death hanging over the sick woman.

"Meretaten," she ventured, "the gods will not punish you for following your physician's advice. Once you are strong and healthy you can try again for a child."

Turning sad eyes to her Nana, Meretaten said "I have lost three other children within the first months of conceiving. This is the longest I have managed to carry a child. I cannot give up now."

Tiya could think of nothing to say. At that moment the bed chamber door opened. It was the King.

"Forgive me, Mother, for not being able to meet

you on arrival. Further trouble in our conquered states! How is my girl?" smiled the King as he reached the bed. Meretaten looked up at him then turned away to hide the tears rolling down her face.

"I am a disappointment to you, Father. I ought to have been able to give you a son. I am truly sorry."

"I will not listen to such talk. You are your mother's daughter, you can never disappoint me. I am proud of your fighting spirit but it saddens me to see you so unwell. Will you not reconsider and let Ir-en relieve you of the child?"

Her head still turned away, she replied "No, Father. My fate is sealed. Either I have this child or die in the attempt."

The King turned to his mother. "You must be tired. Why don't you rest for a while in your quarters. The evening meal will be served soon. I will stay with Meretaten. The maids will soon be in to prepare her for the night. Don't be concerned. Someone is here throughout the night in case Meretaten needs anything."

As Tiya rose to leave her son took her hands. "Thank you, Mother, for coming."

She smiled, tenderly touching his tired face and left.

Chapter 21

Two days later Meretaten's condition worsened. As a result of toxin build up, due to the lack of water and nourishment, her vital organs started shutting down one by one. Ir-en, on visiting the Princess before retiring for the evening, could see she may not survive the night. He listened but could not hear the baby's heartbeat. He rang Meretaten's bell and sent messengers to the King and Queen to come to their daughter's quarters. He gave the patient a potion to ease her discomfort. Holding her head, he coaxed her to drink the elixir.

The King and Queen arrived together and, for the first time, the Queen saw the condition of her first-born. While not prone to showing any emotion apart from frustration and anger, the Queen was lost for words and wept silently at the sight of her suffering child. The King looked at Ir-en, who shook his head indicating he did not hold out hope for the Princess surviving the night.

"I have given her a potion which will ease any pain she might be in."

The King looked at his daughter. "I should have overridden your wishes, Meretaten," he whispered to her. "I could have saved your life."

His daughter's eyelids fluttered. She was trying to say something. The King put his face close to hers to hear her whisper, "Do not blame yourself, Father. This is my wish, to be with the souls of my dead children and with the gods. Forgive me for leaving you and my sisters."

"Your mother is here," said the King as he indicated to his wife to come near. Nefertiti touched her child's face with a cool hand. Meretaten managed to open her eyes again. She smiled at her mother, closed her eyes and stopped breathing.

Tiya was informed the next morning and was allowed to see her granddaughter before the embalmers took the body. The young woman looked at peace, with a smile on her face.

Tiya blessed her grandchild and said a prayer for her safe journey into the next world. She had seen so much death in her time. The pain is unbearable when it is a young soul that has flown. She recollected how desolate she felt at the loss of her first-born, Tutmosis, and then to lose her grandson Smenkhkare, was as much as her heart could handle. The only balm was that they would find happiness in the afterlife.

Meretaten's sisters were happy that she was no longer

suffering but were really devastated to be deprived of her company. She had been like a mother to all of them. They could talk to her about worries and concerns which they would never think to discuss with their mother.

Tiya did her best to divert the bereaved sisters. Despite the sad circumstances Tiya thanked the gods for allowing her to get acquainted with her remaining grand-daughters Mekeaten, Neferernaten, Neferneferuraten called Neferaten, Septepanraten and the youngest Ankhersenpaaten called Ankhen.

Tiya admitted to herself her youngest granddaughter was her favourite. She was loving, obliging and naturally intelligent. She seemed most affected by the loss of her elder sister. Hence Tiya spent more time with her.

Since the villa was only the other side of the city, frequent letters had been sent and received. Tiya was comforted to know all was well at home. The seventy days funeral process for Meretaten had commenced. Tiya, feeling homesick, stayed for a further thirty days after Meretaten's passing and then sought her son's permission to take Ankhen with her when she returned home and to keep her at least until her sister's funeral rites were completed.

The King consulted his Queen before giving his mother an answer. Since the death of her first born, Nefertiti seemed to have lost her fight and verve. She was instinctively unhappy to let her youngest go but accepted her husband's suggestion that it would be better for Ankhen, by reason of her age and sensibilities, not to be at the Palace at this time. Thus it was, some thirty five days after leaving the villa, Tiya returned with a playmate for Tut.

During her time at the palace Zelda blossomed into a confident handmaiden. She looked after both Tiya and her ancient maid, Edfu.

She had to deal with the palace cooks to ensure Tiya's food was boiled with herbs for flavour; with the laundry servants to ensure Tiya's clothes were washed carefully; with the cleaning servants to ensure they dusted properly every day and the toilets were cleaned and the buckets emptied and returned as soon after breakfast as possible. Zelda's eyes had acquired a brightness not there before. Even her hair seemed to bounce with new life.

In fact Zelda had done such a good job Tiya decided to keep her as her handmaiden when they returned to the villa. She would still have her faithful Edfu with her but only for companionship.

Maya will just have to train one of the other young

servants in the household to assist her, thought Tiya.

There had been no outings for Tut. His Nana had said she could not bear the worry while she was away from the villa. He had spent time doing a painting of the flower garden for his Nana which was waiting for her in her resting room. He had been kept busy learning his letters and numbers, the names of the months and the problems caused by the difference between the lunar and solar calendars. He was told his Nana was returning but nothing was said about Ankhen.

Nakht had been a regular visitor and Tut's skill with the bow and arrow had improved considerably. Nakht taught Tut the basics of running, to build up stamina and of wrestling and hand-to-hand combat which kept the young Prince occupied within the walls of the villa.

Manetho also made time for Tut when Nakht could not visit. He taught Tut the art of planting and taking care of flowers, fruit and vegetables. The large vegetable patch to the rear of the villa became a firm favourite with Tut. He was fascinated by the fact that a tiny seed, put in the earth, could grow into something nutritious as well as delicious to eat. He was given a patch in which to grow his own vegetables and greens.

On receiving Tiya's letter, Maya started reviewing the girls of the household who were aged ten and over to ascertain which would be good candidates for training as handmaidens to assist with looking after both Tut and Ankhen.

After much thought Maya decided on two girls, Mira and Mina, identical twin sisters of twelve. Their mother was the senior kitchen maid and their father the under-gardener who had accompanied Tut and Manetho.

Needless to say their parents were proud to have their girls chosen to work in the main house. Both girls were quick learners and eager to please.

Tiya was sad to leave the palace without saying goodbye to Ir-en but it could not be helped. He was away on state business. The King had lent his services to one of his favoured diplomats. She was also sad that at no time during her stay did Nefertiti make an effort to meet her. In fact Tiya had not had so much as a glimpse of her daughter-in-law. Her son never made mention of his wife and Tiya thought it best not to say anything either. Her heart went out to her son. He seemed beset not only with family concerns but also with weighty matters of state.

Manetho arrived at the palace at the agreed time with a couple of carts for the luggage and a coach for the women. They reached the villa late in the afternoon. Tiya could not believe how good it felt to be back in her own home, surrounded by her own belongings. Tut was surprised and delighted to see Ankhen step out of the coach. He looked up at Maya questioningly.

"Do you remember that girl, Tut?"

"She looks familiar but I don't know why."

"She came with her older sister and the King when he visited you on your fourth birthday. The two of you got on well. She is your half -sister Ankhen, and will be staying with us for a while."

Maya took the Princess and her handmaiden up to their quarters. It had been decided that the Princess was too young and too upset to be left in the guest quarters so she and her maid were given rooms just along from Tut and Maya. Ankhen's handmaiden, Peseshet, was introduced to Mira, the elder of the twins, who would be assisting her in looking after the Princess.

Maya instructed Mira to bring Ankhen to Tut's dining room once she had freshened up and to look after her handmaiden by introducing her to the other servants and explaining to her how this, much smaller household, functioned.

Before long Maya, with the help of Swnwt and the younger twin Mina, was supervising the evening meal. Tut invited her to eat with them but Maya declined, explaining she was going to take her evening meal later with Tiya.

Tut found Ankhen really easy to talk to. In between mouthfuls of bread and honey he told her about his horse Safia.

"She is not my horse exactly but I am allowed to ride her. She is pure white and nuzzles me on my neck with her soft velvety nose. Tomorrow I will show you the vegetable garden," he promised Ankhen. "Maybe Manetho will give you a patch of your own to grow whatever vegetables you want. There are so many different types of spinach and lettuces and each has its own distinctive flavour."

So he continued with Ankhen smiling and nodding at everything he said. She thought him a very pretty boy and a novelty since she had always been the youngest. Here, she was the older one.

Tut came to just above her waist when they stood together. She could not help feeling she wanted to look after him. She had never experienced such an emotion before.

So the days flew by and before long it was time for Ankhen to return to the palace. She did not want to leave Tut. She had come to love him with all her young heart.

She had spent more time outdoors than ever before in her life and was a healthy golden colour. Tiya was pleased to note the girl's arms and legs had more flesh on than when she arrived and her cheeks had a healthy glow.

On Ankhen's return the Queen also noted, with disapproval, the changes in her daughter.

"You are the colour of a *fellahin*! Did your grandmother not keep you out of the sun?"

"No," replied Ankhen. "The Prince and I had lessons in the mornings and spent the afternoons playing in the gardens."

"I should not have allowed you to go. Your looks have been spoilt. Go to your quarters; maybe your sisters can do something to restore your complexion."

Ankhen could not understand her mother's displeasure and longed for the peaceful and loving atmosphere of the villa.

On meeting her father on her return, Ankhen asked him whether she could accompany him to Tut's sixth birthday which he readily agreed to. In the meantime she would, she decided, have to survive on the memories of her time with Tut at the villa.

As Tut's sixth birthday loomed Tiya was distressed at the thought of losing Tut and Maya; Maya was worried at the thought of leaving Tiya and having to cope with palace intrigue after having been away from it for so long and Swnwt was ill at ease at the prospect of being in close proximity to the Queen and what she may be commanded to do to harm the Prince.

END OF BOOK ONE

Dear Reader

If you have enjoyed reading this book, then please tell your friends and relatives and leave a review on Amazon.
Thank you.

About the Author

Apart from writing, as part of her job as a graduate local authority and then Private Client lawyer, the author fell in love with Tutankamun when she saw the treasures from his tomb at the Cairo Museum in Egypt over 20 years ago and started researching life in Egypt at that time.

On retiring from her Practice she was finally able to devote time to her writing. Research and findings of modern technology have made the telling of this story of the life of Pharaoh Tutankamun possible.

The author's hobbies include painting, walking, swimming, cooking and socialising with friends and family.

To keep up to date on ADP Sorisi's writing and follow her on social media please go to https://www.facebook.com/ADP-Sorisi-400585110274990/?fref=ts